Cross My Heart

By Janet Miller
Illustrated By Martin Rose

A Hodgepog Book

Hodgepog Books acknowledges the ongoing support of the Canada Council for the Arts.

Editors: Luanne Armstrong, and Dorothy Woodend

Cover design and inside layout by Linda Uyehara Hoffman
Set in Arquitectura and ITC Esprit in Quark XPress 4.1
Printed at Hignell Book Printing

A Hodgepog Book for Kids

Published in Canada by Hodgepog Books,
3476 Tupper Street
Vancouver, BC
V5Z 3B7
Telephone (604) 874-1167
Email: woodend@telus.net

National Library of Canada Cataloguing in Publication Data
Miller, Janet.
    Cross my heart

    ISBN 0-9730831-0-7

    I. Title.

PS8576.I5388C76   2002   jC813'.6   C2002-910955-8
PZ7.M6162Cr   2002

The Canada Council | Le Conseil des Arts
for the Arts | du Canada

Cross My Heart

Table of Contents

Chapter 1
STOP THE BUS

It was March and the snow was almost gone from the school yard at Pemberton Meadows Elementary. At lunch time Julie had been turning her end of the skipping rope. The girl whose turn it was to skip had faced Julie.

And then between jumps as though it was an old skipping rhyme, the girl said, "My-mom-says-your-mom-is-going-to-die."

Julie felt a huge shock roll through her body. She stopped turning the rope. The girl added, "What are you going to do when your mom dies?" Julie wanted to give the girl a huge shove. Instead she threw down her end of the skipping rope and ran through the mud and piles of snow to the back of the school and sat on some old steps where no one could see her. She took in great breaths of air. She could feel her heart pounding in her chest. She didn't go back into the school when the bell rang.

Miss Hendricks, the teacher, came clomping through the mud in a pair of big boots she must have borrowed from one of the older boys. The boots she usually wore were see-through rubber that she slipped on over her shoes. Julie shook her head to say "No," when Miss Hendricks asked her if she wanted to talk. The teacher's glasses hung from a delicate silver chain around her neck. She had her overcoat on top of the sweater she always wore slung over her shoulders with only the top button done up. She snugged her coat and sweater tighter around her shoulders and sat beside

Julie on the step. When she put her arm around Julie's shoulders, Julie could smell her perfume. They sat quietly for a few minutes.

"I took over this job from your mother, you know, Julie. She came here straight out of teacher's college."

Julie didn't say anything but she imagined—as she had done before—how her mother must have looked up at the front of the classroom, writing on the green blackboard with her beautiful slanted handwriting, wearing prettier clothes than she wore when she was at home on the farm.

It was chilly and when Miss Hendricks said, "Shall we go in and warm up, dear?" Julie agreed. She found it hard to concentrate on her arithmetic lesson that afternoon. She

kept thinking about what the girl had said and wondering if it could be true.

That afternoon Julie was the first on the bus. She waited, perched on the edge of her seat, holding her breath and her lunch kit.

Julie MacFarlane was going to get off the school bus at the wrong place. On purpose.

That very morning her father had waited at the road by their farm for the bus with her and had told Mr. Smokey Woodburn, the driver, "Can you drop Julie at Mary Margaret's tonight again, Smokey?"

"Sophie not feeling well, Duncan?" Smokey had asked.

Julie's father nodded.

Mary Margaret Sorenson lived just down the road and was Julie's father's old cousin. Julie was not at all keen to have to go there after school. Julie knew that her mother hadn't been well. For months now her mother had barely been able to do all the jobs she used to do. Neither of Julie's parents appeared to be bothered that the farmhouse was messy most of the time, and lots of meals now were just a peanut butter sandwich and a cup of tea. For the first time in Julie's ten years they ate store-bought cookies and white bread because her mother wasn't feeling up to baking anymore.

The bus rounded the last corner and bumped along the road getting closer to her farm. She leapt from her seat and ran to the front screaming, "Stop! Stop! Stop the bus! Let me OFF!"

The other kids watched from their seats, wide-eyed

with admiration. No one except Julie would ever yell at Mr Smokey Woodburn. Mr. Smokey Woodburn geared down and put on the screechy brakes.

"But, Julie," he said patiently. "Your dad told me you're to go to Mary Margaret Sorenson's because your mom's … ah-h-h … not so well today."

Julie hopped down onto the first step by the door. Then she turned and faced him, fists on her hips. Just because he'd known her since she was born and was a friend of her father's, it didn't mean that he could tell her where she should get off the school bus. And just to make sure that he didn't smile at her like he did some days, she scowled at him in a terrible way.

He let out a loud breath and muttered, "Julie MacFarlane, you are a stubborn little girl ..." But he leaned forward and pushed the silver lever that swung open the door. Julie flung herself down the last two steps and off the bus.

"And there's NOTHING wrong with my MOTHER!" she yelled at the bus as it pulled back onto the gravel road. "She's fine. She's just fine. You don't know anything about her." Julie felt so mad that she wanted to throw rocks at the back of the yellow school bus. She glared after it as it drove down the windy road in the middle of the Pemberton Valley. Tree-covered mountains rose up on both side of the flat farmland. Far in the distance, in the direction that the bus had taken, Mount Currie spread its snowy bulk from one side of the valley to the other. The afternoon sun touched only the top peaks of Mount Currie. The air had a chill to it.

Dogeez waited on the other side of the road. He wagged his short stubby tail and panted, wiggling his whole fluffy grey body. The tips of his ears folded over to the front and shaggy tufts of hair—eyebrows, Julie called them—hung over his deep brown eyes. She didn't feel like playing today but Dogeez was always in such a good mood so she talked to him anyway. "You're a real mutt-and-a-half, Dogeez." She patted his head and scratched behind his ears. "I have to talk to mother." Julie could not think of what it was that she would ask mother.

They picked their way through mud and snow patches on the way to the farmhouse. The MacFarlane farm was a gloomy place in the late winter. The house looked old with its grey shingles and sharply pitched roof. There was also a woodshed with a sloped roof that leaned against the house and a chicken house that stood by itself close to where the garden grew in the summer. Past the garden was an old house where no one had lived for years. Beyond the old house lay the fields.

The words of the girl at school went around and around in Julie's head. My-mom-says, my-mom-says.

Dogeez stayed on the porch when Julie went into the house. He was an outside dog and never came into the house. He slept on an old ripped-up blanket on the porch with the cats at night.

Julie tiptoed into the house with her dirty boots on and peeked into the living room. A low fire glowed in the fireplace. Mother was curled asleep on the sofa under the butterfly quilt that Grandma had brought the last time she had visited. Julie didn't want to wake her, so instead blew a kiss across the room and imagined it landing on mother's pale cheek. Mother's dark hair was sleek and smooth, not at all like Julie's sandy mop that tended to sproing up in wings above her ears and fall over her forehead whether she wanted bangs or not. Julie and her mother had both taken to wearing a shorter cut these days because mother said it was easier to manage.

Julie could see the clumps of mud she had dropped on the kitchen floor but she didn't stop to clean them up. She closed the front door softly behind her and tried to think where her father might be. "Let's find him, Dogeez." They walked past the chicken house and down towards the barn.

The cows gave birth to their calves this time of year.

Every night Father would write down how many had been born that day and if they were bulls or heifers. Julie found her father as he drove the tractor and hay wagon out of the mucky barn yard on his way to feed the yearling steers in the field. The cows and new calves were in a different field below the barn. He waved at her and stopped the tractor so that she could climb up onto the wagon. She knew she should have changed out of her school clothes. Out in the field Father shut the tractor off and joined her on the wagon.

"You didn't fancy going to Mary Margaret's, eh? She takes some getting used to, I grant you that." He forked hay off the sides for the jostling steers. "We'll have to mosey over there later and tell her you're okay." Julie kicked the last bits of hay off the wagon with the toe of her boot. Her father was leaning his hands and chin on the hay fork and looking over the animals.

"Father," she said, "a girl at school said ... she said ..." Julie didn't want to say the words out loud. She couldn't say them. The air was cold and crisp, and she watched steam rise from the backs of the milling steers around the wagon. Tears squeezed out of the corners of Julie's eyes and began to roll down her cheeks. "Is mother going to ... will she be okay or will ..."

There was a long silence. "We don't know, Julie." Father's voice was deep and sounded as sad as Julie had felt all afternoon. "The doctor told her that her heart is faulty ... weakening. She doesn't have a lot of strength. I'm hoping she can rest and ..." His voice trailed off.

"What would we do, Father? If.... she. ...."

Another silence. "We would carry on our lives. Somehow. But our hearts, they'd be broken."

Julie and Father sat on the edge of the wagon with their feet dangling down. Dogeez lay between them. They didn't say anything else. When one steer or another came in close to sniff and snort at them—looking for more hay—they swung their feet up, halfheartedly, to kick the steers in the noses but the young and frisky steers always jumped back in time.

Chapter 2
THE NEWSPAPER ARTICLE

Before Julie's mother got so sick, Julie's father used to go around to the back of the house and come in the basement door. A clothes rack on pulleys was rigged up beside the wood furnace for his wet clothes: jackets, socks and wool pants. This winter he came into the house a lot during the day to see if mother was all right. He came in the front door to the kitchen with his muddy boots on. Snow melted and dripped onto the linoleum and great chunks of mud fell off his boots.

"I need to warm up a bit," he'd say. "Cold as blazes out there. Let's have a cup of tea, Sophie." Julie saw her mother smile her tired smile and touch his cold whiskery cheek with the back of her fingers. After a while Mother began keeping a full pot of tea ready on the stove top.

Neighbours and relatives came by with food all ready to put in the oven. "Won't stay a minute, Sophie," they said. "Heard you've been feeling poorly. Just thought I'd drop by with this extra pie I had on my hands." When she got home from school Julie would run into the kitchen to see if anyone had left anything really yummy.

Auntie Francine, who was her father's older sister—and who had an important job as secretary-treasurer of the Dyking District—started coming Saturdays to boss them around. She made Julie's mother take long naps. Auntie Francine complained about the mud that Father tracked in from outside. She said it made the kitchen floor look like the dirt floor of a trapper's cabin. As she went from room to room she grumbled as she scooped up dirty clothes. She shoved the clothes in the wringer washer without even sorting them into piles. Julie knew how to help with the laundry but Auntie Francine just said, "Out of my way, kiddo." Auntie Francine seemed to think that children were a big nuisance.

One Saturday in April, Auntie Francine drove Julie and her mother down to the village to get groceries from the Valley Food Mart. While they waited in the check-out line behind Auntie Francine, Julie ran her finger along the chocolate bar display. Mother took a Toronto newspaper from the rack and flipped through it.

Suddenly she exclaimed, "Oh, goodness gracious!" and dropped the newspaper. The pages went flying all over the floor. Julie couldn't imagine what was happening. Auntie Francine was at Mother's side with her arm around her. Julie couldn't tell if Mother was laughing or crying. Her shoulders were shaking and she was bent over the shopping cart, grasping its metal sides with both her hands. People in the line-up behind them were asking what the fuss was all about.

"Francine ...," her mother's voice came out in a whisper. "The paper! Read the paper!" Auntie Francine frowned at the people gathering around and then bent over to gather up the scattered pages.

*   *   *

Slumped in the back seat of Auntie Francine's old car on the drive home up the valley, Julie felt quite put out. They had left the store in such a hurry that she hadn't remembered to ask for a chocolate bar like she'd planned. She folded her arms across her chest. There's never chocolate in the house now that Mother doesn't bake anymore, she thought. She stared out the window and concentrated on counting cows in the fields. She told herself that if she could count 100 cows before they got home there might be a chance that her mother would at least have bought baking chocolate with the groceries.

Chapter 3
JULIE FINDS OUT

That night after supper Julie fidgeted in her chair at the kitchen table, trying to concentrate on her arithmetic homework. Because it was Saturday she didn't see why her homework was so important. She could do it tomorrow. But her father had insisted. Then he had gone into the living room with a cup of tea for Mother. Julie could hear her mother reading out loud. Julie crept over to the living room door and listened.

Mother had a newspaper on her lap. "I'll write to Doctor Pardon tomorrow and ask him what he knows about this new procedure. Imagine, Duncan, those doctors in Toronto are cutting right into people's chests and repairing their hearts. How I found that article I'll just never know. It was right there staring up at me."

"It's a miracle, Sophie," Father said. "It was meant to be."

"I wonder if they'll start doing this operation in Vancouver in time for me ... for us." Mother's voice trailed off.

Then Julie heard her father's voice again, "It'll happen, Sophie. It's 1956, remember. There's all those fancy hospitals and doctors in Vancouver. We've just got to keep your ol' ticker ticking until they're ready for you. Though maybe we should let them practice a few times on somebody else first."

"Oh, Duncan," Mother said, laughing a little, "the day they call me, I'll go for it."

"They'll call, Sophie. They'll call."

Julie felt a wave of fear wash over her whole body. She staggered back and leaned against the kitchen table, breathing heavily. Who was going to cut open Mother's chest? Who was going to call? She shoved her arithmetic text hard across the table and it fell with a crash to the floor. She was crying now with huge sobs that hurt her throat. Why was Mother's heart broken? Julie ran from the kitchen and dashed up the stairway, scrambling on all fours. Her bedroom door slammed shut behind her. She gave it a good kick. Now her foot hurt and she cried even louder. She fell face first across her bed and wept.

She heard her parents coming slowly up the stairs. They talked in low voices outside her door, then the door creaked open. The bed bounced just a little so Julie could tell that it was her mother who had sat down.

Julie sniffled and turned over. She looked at Mother, sitting there on the edge of the bed with her shoulders slumped and her hands limp on her lap. Mother's pale blue eyes met Julie's. "I'll tell you about my heart ... Slide over, sweetie, and let me lie down." Julie made room for her mother, then tugged the quilt from the bottom of the bed up over both of them.

Her mother told her about how, as a child in Saskatchewan in the late 1920s, she'd had rheumatic fever and nearly died and it had somehow damaged her heart. She'd been pretty much okay until the last year or so. When she had come here to Pemberton as a teacher she was fine, and when she got married to Julie's father she was fine, but now her heart was starting to wear out. Something called valves were leaking and her heart wasn't doing its proper job of pumping blood and a good supply of oxygen through her veins and arteries.

Mother took Julie's arm and gently traced a finger along the blue lines just under the skin, between Julie's wrist and elbow. "These are your veins," Mother said.

Last year when Mother had gone to see Doctor Pardon in Vancouver, he had told her that there was nothing he could do to help. She would just get weaker and weaker. But now she'd read in that Toronto newspaper about some new operation that could maybe fix her heart.

When Mother finished talking, she sighed in a sad quiet way and snuggled a little closer. Julie felt her head bursting with all this new information. She lay perfectly still for a long time, then peeked at her mother. She was fast asleep. Julie needed to talk to her father. She waited a few more minutes, then she slipped out of bed and tiptoed out of the room. She almost stumbled over him, sitting in the dark on the top step, his back propped against the wall. His arms were folded across his knees and his head rested on his arms. He's sleeping too, thought Julie. He'll fall down the stairs if he doesn't watch out.

"Father," Julie said, tapping him gently on the arm. "Father, you're sleeping in the wrong place."

Father's head came up and he blinked his eyes, "Your mother …"

"She fell asleep on my bed," Julie said. "She told me about her heart, Father. She can sleep with me tonight. You go on down to bed."

He rose, hugged Julie and started down the stairs.

"Father," Julie called, leaning over the banister. Her father stopped and looked up at her from the stairwell. "She'll be okay," Julie whispered down at him. She placed her hand against her chest, making an X shape with her finger. "Cross my heart and hope to die." She'd heard that somewhere and she knew it meant a promise that would be kept.

Chapter 4
SPRINGTIME

When spring came to Pemberton, Mother was so sick she hardly got out of bed anymore. The snow was gone. The mud on the paths and the road had dried out. Julie could wear shoes to school instead of gum boots with heavy socks. Grass had popped up everywhere and turned the cow pastures and the school playing field a soft green. When she was outside in the sunshine with Dogeez at her side, Julie could almost forget about Mother's problems. For a little while.

Father had his hands full with the springtime farmwork of getting the fields ready for planting the crops. He grew potatoes which were sold as seed to other farmers and oats that were grown to feed their own cattle He spent his days plowing and discing. Up and down. Back and forth. Over and over. Julie liked the criss-cross patterns the tractor and the machinery made on the fields.

Doctor Pardon had written to Mother. He said that he expected to schedule her for heart surgery before the end of the summer. "With your general good health and youthfulness, the Medical Board sees you as a good prospect for surgery," he'd written.

Father said everything was arranged. The people who owned the Valley Food Mart were the only ones in Pemberton who had a telephone so the doctor was going to call them and leave a message. Then Mother would go on the train to Vancouver to Grandma's little house on Broughton

Street and wait.

Mother told Julie, "Your grandmother's house is just a skip and a jump from St. Paul's Hospital." And St. Paul's was where Mother was going to have the heart surgery.

Julie knew that she was going to have to go and stay at Mary Margaret and Svend Sorenson's until the end of the school year whether she wanted to or not. And Father—he had to stay home on the farm and look after the animal and the crops.

They looked over a diagram of a heart that Doctor Pardon had sent. Mother said, "This little pipe thing, see where it goes into the heart muscle? There's a valve right there. In my heart that's the part that's not working. The doctor has to patch it up so it doesn't leak so badly."

Father leaned back in his chair, "Julie, you remember that old inner tube you used up at Mosquito Lake? And how we fixed it up? Dr. Excuse-me ... pardon me, what's his name again?" He laughed at his own joke.

A little smile flickered across Mother's face. "You're a silly man, Duncan."

Father continued, "Dr. Pardon-me won't be using glue and a rubber patch but it's not so very different. It's a repair job that's needed here."

Julie stared at the diagram and tried to say the words out loud, "Mitral, chamber, tricuspid, valve." She let out a big breath and put her small hand over her mother's. "Too bad we can't send just your heart out to get fixed."

"I am my heart, honey," her mother said quietly.

Chapter 5
GRANDMA COMES TO HELP

At the begining of May, Grandma came on the train from Vancouver. "Hel-l-lo, my dar-r-ling," she said as she stepped onto the station platform. She put down her two matching suitcases and gave Julie an enormous hug. "Gracious. You're as tall as I am." Grandma was very small and her silvery grey hair was short and curlier than Julie had ever seen it before. "I've had myself a permanent," she announced as she took off her blue felt hat. "It's a miracle of modern times. I wake up in the morning and my hair is already ready. Where's that handsome father of yours and that dusty old rattle-trap he drives?"

In the cab of the truck on the drive up the valley Grandma kept up a steady chatter. She didn't wait for answers from whoever she was talking to.

"Well, Duncan, I know that you and Sophie think you can do without me but I simply had to come. There's nothing that keeps me in town, you know. Nothing except my bridge and book club and volunteering at the library." Grandma counted on her fingers. "Oh and, of course, I visit the shut-ins at the lodge on Wednesdays. Lonely old folk they are. But other than that … No, I just had to come."

Grandma fussed over Mother a great deal and kept herself busy all the time. When she sat down, she said, "I'll just rest my tired feet and have a nice hot cuppa tea." She had brought her own quilted tea cosy for Mother's old brown betty pot. "Truth is, I don't think much of this well water you drink here." Her grey knitting needles clicked and flashed. "Come sit with me, puddin'-cakes. It's time you learned the purl stitch."

One afternoon when Mother lay down for her nap Grandma called to Julie, "Come, Mary-Mary-Quite-Contrary." Grandma closed the screen door quietly behind her. "Let's go see how the garden grows. I saw some lovely narcissus poking their pretty yellow heads up. Down there beside that little house at the bottom of the garden."

"That was the farmhouse in the old days," Julie told Grandma, "before our house got built. Father's Granny lived there. Maybe she planted the flowers."

"Julie," Grandma said as they walked through the scruffy remains of last year's garden, "did you know that your mother had rheumatic fever when she was your age. When she was better we left the prairies and came out west." Grandma stopped and pushed her toe against a lump of dirt. "It will forever hang over my head, that illness and the damage it did to her heart. Although, of course, we didn't know at the time. Had no idea. We were just thankful that she got better." Julie slipped her arm through Grandma's.

As they walked around the outside of the old house Grandma bent every few steps and pulled up weeds in the overgrown flowerbeds. "Some serious weeding would make a world of difference. Look, a thistle." Grandma made her tsk-tsk sound. "Such a shame. I'd be at that nasty thistle with a hoe, mark my words."

At the back corner of the old house, in the shade, a spout came down off the roof into a covered wooden barrel. "A rain barrel," Grandma said, delighted. "Water from a rain barrel is excellent for thirsty plants. And," she said, fluffing up her droopy hairdo with her weed-stained hands, "it's very good for washing hair."

They came to the front door of the old house. "Shall we go in?" Grandma asked, turning the doorknob and not waiting for an answer from Julie. Inside the house, soft-fuzzy daylight shone in through the dusty windows. Julie felt like sneezing. Grandma breathed on a corner of her apron and rubbed a spot clean on the glass. "You'd sit yourself down for breakfast, here." There was no furniture where Grandma was pointing. "And lo and behold, there that lovely mountain would be, right through the window. I wonder if it has a name?"

"Mount Currie," Julie said. She breathed on her two pointer fingers and rubbed spots clean on the window for each of her eyes to see out.

"Hmmmmm, you'd want to stick with sheer drapes ..." Grandma turned around in a complete circle, "to get the most of the view and the light. Don't you think?" Julie had never seen a grandma playing house before.

Grandma zig-zagged her finger along the dusty window sill leaving a clean wavy trail. "A bit of elbow grease is all this house needs. And indoor plumbing, of course."

Julie looked carefully at Grandma's elbows but she couldn't for the life of her figure out where the grease would come from.

On the days when Father used the manure spreader on the fields and made himself and the whole farm very stinky, Grandma served the mid-day meal with the kitchen door propped open and all the windows as wide open as they would go. She said that she couldn't understand how the smell of the cow manure could cling like it did.

"It's got to be done, Granny," Father told her. "It'll only smell for a few more days." He laughed, "Wait until I do the garden tomorrow, then you'll really smell something."

Grandma made a little huffy sound with her mouth. Julie had an idea that Grandma might be out of sorts because her hair was losing its curl. It got straighter and straighter every time she washed it.

"And Duncan," Grandma said. "Why do you insist on calling me Granny?"

Father rubbed his fingers through his hair then braced both of his hands against the edge of the table. "Well ..." he started. "Well, when I was a little boy my Granny lived near us. Always lived near us, you know, in that little house just a stone's throw away. I must have said the word Granny a hundred times a day. She passed on when I was still a kid. My own mother didn't last long enough to be a Granny. When I married Sophie and you showed up, all tiny and beautiful and business-like, I just couldn't help myself. You were Granny." He shrugged his shoulders.

"Oh," said Grandma. And in a soft voice, "I see."

Chapter 6
THE ALBATROSS

When the bell rang after lunch on a warm day in late May at Pemberton Meadows Elementary School, all the children lined up on the cement area waiting to go back into the classroom. The Grade Ones were first in the line, then the Twos, Threes and Fours, with just a couple of children in each grade. Then came Julie and the other Grade Fives and finally the Sixes who had no girls at all and were only boys with pants too short for their long legs.

Although there were two classrooms in the school, one of them stood empty for lack of students and Miss Hendricks taught all of the children in one room. The empty classroom had rows of desks and the school piano was kept there. All six grades were taught different lessons at the same time.

Today Miss Hendricks came out onto the school porch carrying a wooden chair. "Here," she said to one of the Grade Six boys, "take my chair, please. We'll be reading outside today. Go ahead, children. You may run."

They ran lickety-split around the side of the school. The biggest boys were in the lead. Because they arrived at the reading spot first, they got to sit with their backs leaning against the board fence. The younger children sprawled on the grass around the teacher's empty chair. Miss Hendricks smiled when she came around the corner and saw all twenty-three of them waiting.

She settled on her chair and opened her book at the bookmark. The children wiggled about getting even more comfortable.

"'The Rhyme of the Ancient Mariner.' Now where did we leave that old sailor? Oh yes, here we are." She began to read.

Julie lay flat with her stomach against the warm grass. She rested her head on her crossed arms. She tried to concentrate on the words of the story, but it was too hard to think about anything except how sick her mother was. It filled her whole head.

Miss Hendricks read about a huge bird, an albatross that followed the ancient mariner's ship. Julie knew about ravens and baldheaded eagles and great blue herons and cranes. But this albatross seemed to be much bigger than any Pemberton bird.

When one of the Grade Ones asked whether it was a real bird or not, Miss Hendricks stopped reading and said, "The albatross is real all right. It's a huge white seabird with a very wide wing span. It can fly long distances out to sea without touching land. It's real, but it also represents fate and destiny." She checked a page of handwritten notes. "The dictionary tells us that fate is a power thought to control all events and impossible to resist, and destiny is that which happens to a person or thing, thought of as determined in advance by fate. In another way I suppose it has a lot to do with good luck and bad luck, too. And you all know what those mean."

Julie looked down into the grass in front of her nose. There was the tiniest bee in proper bee colours, orange with black stripes. He was so small his buzz was almost impossible to hear. She hoped he knew how to get himself off the ground and into the air where he'd be safer. She cupped her hands on either side of the little bee to protect him and watched him as he crawled slowly up a blade of grass. At the top he rubbed his feet together and wiggled his feelers.

Miss Hendricks read about how the ancient mariner cursed the slimy, ugly sea creatures around his ship. Maybe he should just look at them really closely, Julie thought, and they wouldn't seem so bad. Like this little bee of mine. And then the teacher's voice said that the mariner blessed the sea creatures! He blessed them instead of not liking them! Just like I thought he should. Julie's little bee stretched out his wings and flew off, bumbling through the air just barely above the level of the grass. With a few clever turns this way and that, he managed not to bump into any of the children or the legs of the teacher's chair. He's doing fine, she thought. He's not much of a bee, but he seems to be lucky. She tried a new word. Maybe it's his destiny.

After the reading time was over and all the children had straggled back into the classroom, Julie sat at her desk and gazed out the window. A bird flittered from a tree branch across the road and landed on top of the monkey bars, resting. He held some dry grass in his beak. She wondered why birds didn't just remember where their last year's nest was and use that one again instead of building a new one each spring.

There was dust rising from the road, and then a blue truck came slowly around the corner and drove towards the school. Mary Margaret and Svend had an old blue truck like that one, she thought. Now it was getting closer to the school and Julie could see that someone very short, like Svend, was driving and there was a black and white dog sitting on the front seat beside him. Mary Margaret never sat in the front of the truck because she was sure that it was much safer in the back where she could jump out if they went in the ditch. Julie ran over to the window and leaned her forehead against the glass.

Svend pulled off the road and came to a bumpy stop right in front of the school. Mary Margaret sat perfectly still on her spare tire seat in the back as the road dust settled around her. She wore a shapeless felt hat to keep God's creatures, like bugs, from flying into her ears. Svend got out and slammed the truck door, dusting off his overalls. They both wore plaid jackets, like always. He walked around the back and pulled open the tail gate. He took a block of wood out of the back of the truck and placed it on the ground. Mary Margaret rose from her seat and took his outstretched hand. She stepped gingerly down onto the block of wood and then onto the ground. By now all the children in the classroom were watching through the window. Even Miss Hendricks was staring at the visitors.

"It's my ... it's my ... my relatives," Julie blurted. "It's the Sorensons. Miss Hendricks, I'll have to go now. They've come about my mother." She ran out of the classroom.

"Wait, Julie. You mustn't ... oh ... Grade Sixes, you're in charge." Miss Hendricks got to the front door just behind Julie and followed her down the sidewalk as the Sorensons came through the schoolyard gate.

Svend smiled solemnly at Julie but didn't say a single word. Mary Margaret put her hands on Julie's shoulders. "It's your mother, child. Dr. Pardon called and she's getting ready to leave for the train to Vancouver. You must spend some time with her before she goes. Only the Good Lord knows when she'll be back."

Julie sucked in her breath and her heart banged in her chest. She ran for the truck. The Sorensons hurried along behind her.

"We went down to the village to buy chicken feed at the Co-op. Then the Good Lord saw fit to direct us to the Valley Food Mart just when Dr. Pardon called," Mary Margaret told Julie breathlessly. "When we went to your place, your father was out somewhere, so your mother said for us to come for you straight away." Mary Margaret opened the passenger door for Julie. "You sit up front with Victor McClusky McGlory and Svend, child." Mary Margaret got into the back and Julie got in the front with Svend and the black and white dog. Svend did a wide U-turn and they started slowly down the valley in a big cloud of dust.

Chapter 7
SPECIAL TEA

As the Sorenson truck stopped at Julie's farmyard, Dogeez came out and ran around and around it barking. He didn't seem to like Victor very much. Victor sat perfectly still on the front seat and looked straight ahead through the windshield. He didn't pay any attention to Dogeez. If Dogeez ever visited Victor's farm, then it was Victor who had to bark and act tough.

Julie leapt out. Mary Margaret, still in the back of the truck, leaned over the side and grabbed hold of Julie's arm, "I won't come in, dear. Your mother is busy getting ready to leave. Go now. Go. The Lord will bless and keep her, Julie Kathleen, all the days of her life." Julie ran to the house. Svend stayed in the driver's seat.

Mary Margaret leaned even futher over the side of the truck and called towards the house, "My prayers will reach you, Sophie." She wiped at her eyes with the sleeve of her jacket and sniffed. "Come, Svend. We must be off. We're late with the chores." Svend backed the truck around and drove off down the road.

Dogeez stopped barking. He came up on the porch and lay down.

After they finished the packing, Grandma, Mother and Julie kept each other company in the living room and waited for Father to come home. Mother lay on the chesterfield with pillows behind her and a blanket tucked around her. Julie sat quietly at the end of the chesterfield with her mother's feet on her lap. She put her arms around Mother's feet and hugged them tight. The luggage was ready and waiting, stacked up in the living room.

Father drove the tractor into the farmyard by the house. He stopped the tractor and climbed off, carefully reached in behind the seat and lifted a silver bucket down and placed it on the grass. Dogeez wandered over and sniffed the bucket. Father patted Dogeez on the head, then came towards the house carrying the bucket.

Grandma had her arms crossed and was watching him through the living room window. "What do you suppose Duncan has brought home, Sophie?"

"Could be almost anything. Let's see—what's he brought home before, Julie? Yellow violets, trilliums from the forest and watercress from the creek by the rockslide." She chuckled and had to catch her breath. "Once he brought us a whole nest of orphaned baby hares. There's no telling what he's brought today."

The front door opened with a bang, "Granny, come take a look at this," he called.

Grandma went out to the kitchen. She peeked into the bucket. "Water. It looks like water, Duncan."

"Yes, water! Excellent, Granny. But not ordinary water. This is the freshest, most oxygen-filled, sweetest water that ever tumbled down a mountainside. Punch Creek water it is. Oxygenated, they call it! Now this will make you a cup of tea to end all cups of tea!"

"Well!" said Grandma, "I never ..."

"Sophie!" Father looked into the living room, "You two

look comfy. Where are the very best teacups in the house?" He put the kettle in the sink and sloshed water from the bucket into it. Straightening up suddenly, he looked across the room at Grandma. "Isn't it kind of early for Julie to be home?" He was already moving towards the living room door where the packed suitcases were piled. "Sophie," he said, and with a few long strides crossed the room. Julie watched him with a gloomy face. She stayed at her spot at the end of the chesterfield and kept hold of Mother's feet on her lap. Father knelt in front of Mother and lay his head on Mother's tummy.

Grandma stayed in the kitchen and fussed with the teapot and the tea cozy. She moved the kettle from the sink to the stove top and set the sugar and milk on the kitchen table after brushing invisible crumbs from the tablecloth.

After a while Father lifted his head. He looked at Mother. Then Julie. Then Mother again.

"Yes, Duncan," said Mother, "the wheels of fate are in motion. We all need that special cup of tea now."

*   *   *

Late in the afternoon Father and Julie drove Mother and Grandma to the train station in Pemberton. Grandma went inside and bought the tickets from the station master, Mr. Clack, behind the wicket. Julie sat between her parents on the wooden bench on the platform. There didn't seem to be anyone else going on the train today.

"Listen for the whistle, Julie," said Father.

"Yes," Mother added. "In the winter, when sound travels more easily we can hear it all the way up at our place, can't we, Julie? Seven miles away. Isn't that something?"

Julie didn't want to hear the train whistle. She wished trains didn't even have whistles.

Grandma came outside and stood in front of the little family. "I've bought your ticket, Sophie. Pemberton to Vancouver. And return." Grandma held Mother's train ticket tightly in her hand. Like it was worth a million dollars.

Chapter 8
THE GRASS HOUSE

Mother and Grandma had been gone for one week and Julie was staying at Mary Margaret's but she still got off the school bus at her own family's farm. As soon as Julie stepped her foot from the yellow school bus onto the gravel of the road outside her family's farm, the crankiness she'd cooked up to get the bus to stop blew off her shoulders like dandelion fluff. She watched the back of the bus drive away and whistled at Dogeez who sat on the other side of the road waiting for her. "Take me to where Father's working," she told him. "Let's go, Mr. Doglette."

"I thought I heard that bus stop," said Father, looking up from the tractor engine he was working on. His face was covered with dirt, and trickles of sweat made wiggly white lines down his cheeks and neck. "You being an awful grouch to that poor Smokey Woodburn again?" He took off his straw hat and wiped his sleeve across his forehead.

Julie knew how busy her father was this time of year. It was the end of May and smack in the middle of potato planting time on their farm. He told her that today his tractor had broken down and he'd had to send the crew home early to Creekside where they lived. He paid Johnson Jackson—one of the men who'd worked for him on the potato planting crew for years—extra to gather up and bring the rest of the crew up the valley and drive them home again at night. If Father didn't get the tractor fixed by dark, he'd have to string up a light from the house and keep on trying.

"Here, Father ..." Julie passed him two left-over cookies from her lunch kit. "Mary Margaret makes them kinda too crunchy." Julie thought about the big soft cookies her mother used to make. Puffed-up cookies that smelled of raisins and molasses.

"I guess poor old Mary Margaret should have had kids to tell her how to do things right." Father put the cookies on the seat of the tractor and wiped his hands on his denim overalls. "And speaking of Mary Margaret Sorenson, she'll be flying around like a chicken with its head cut off when she doesn't see you walking up the road from the bus. She'll think you've fallen in the ditch and drowned yourself." He popped the cookies into his mouth and picked up his wrench again, chewing. "Listen, Julie-Dooley, you keep yourself busy while I finish up here. Gotta see if I can fit this gizmo onto this doodad. Then Dogeez and I will drive you over to Mary Margaret's. Seeing's how she's nice enough to look after you, you should be nice enough to show up. I ..." He turned back to the tractor and bent over the engine, "Maybe she'll give me a bite of supper while I'm there."

Julie liked listening to her father talk. The way he explained things sometimes it sounded like he was thinking out loud.

While she waited for Father, Julie walked into a patch of tall couch-grass beside the tractor. She crawled around on her knees flattening a spot big enough for her and Dogeez to have a tea party.

"There," Julie said to Dogeez, patting a place beside

her. "A jim-dandy grass house, just for us." It was quiet and warm here. She could hear bees buzzing around in the air above them.

She opened up her lunch kit and found a peanut butter sandwich crust. Dogeez took the crust gently from her fingers and gulped it right down without chewing. He lay quietly and watched her with his bright brown eyes. Julie licked the tip of her finger and pushed it down onto the golden brown pieces of cookie in the corner of her lunch kit. When all the crumbs were gone, she licked her finger again and pushed back Dogeez's shaggy eyebrows, so he could see better. The springy hairs flopped back in front of his eyes as soon as she let go.

Julie could hear her father singing in his deep voice, "Everything's go-o-o-oing my wa-a-a-a-ay-ay. Everything's going my wa-a-a-a-ay." She circled her finger around her ear and smiled at Dogeez. "He's just plain crackers, isn't he?" Because if the tractor was broken and Father couldn't fix it, and Mother was not well, how could everything-be-going-his-way? Dogeez wagged his tail.

Tiny green grasshoppers popped up out of the grass and landed on her legs one at a time. When she touched them softly on their behinds, they leapt away with little clicking sounds.

Julie stretched out on the warm grass and leaned her head against Dogeez. She thought about her mother.

She tried hard to remember her mother's face. The eyes were easy, because they were the very same pale blue outlined in black that Julie saw every time she looked in the mirror. Her mother's nose was ... was ... had a sort of a pretty rounded part at the tip. She thought about her mother's face for a long time.

But Mother was so far away now.

Chapter 9
THE LOG HOUSE

From her comfortable place in the grass house, Julie could hear Father's voice calling to her and Dogeez. "Come out of hiding, you two." Julie sat up and rubbed the itchiness from her eyes and face. Dogeez got to his feet and sneezed twice before he trotted off. Julie grabbed her lunch kit and followed his wagging tail along the path through the tall grass. The sun had slid behind the mountain and the air was cooler. Julie was very hungry.

"I'll drive you over to Mary Margaret's now," Father said as Julie and Dogeez appeared, "... if I can remember where my truck is. Parked the silly thing around here somewhere. Should have bought a red one. Would have showed up better. Green truck, green grass, green trees. Boy, I can never find it."

At the entrance to Mary Margaret's farm, Julie got out and lifted the latch of the heavy iron gate. Using both arms she pushed the gate as far open as it would go and held it there with all her might, while Father drove through. He tooted the horn and yelled, "Thank you, Jeeves!" Then Julie hopped her feet up on the bottom bar of the gate and hung on as tight as she could with her arms as the gate swung wildly backwards at a great speed. A cool wind ruffled her hair. The gate slammed to a stop with a huge jolt but Julie didn't fall. She let go and jumped off, lined up the gate with the corner post of the fence and flapped the latch down, then she ran to catch up with Father. He was parking the truck under a big willow tree. The tree branches and leaves hung down like a saggy green tent around the truck. As Father climbed from the front of the truck, he looked down at his dirty hands and arms.

"Not a chance," he said to Julie, turning his hands over one way and then the other. "Not a chance Mary Margaret will let me near the house like this!"

Dogeez stayed in the back of the truck. Victor came out and ran around the truck a few times, barking. But Dogeez stayed low and didn't bark back. He did his best to ignore Victor.

Julie and her father walked up the path towards Mary Margaret's log house. They could hear Mary Margaret's voice before they could see her.

"You stop right there, Duncan MacFarlane. You're not sitting at my kitchen table until you've cleaned up." Pots and pans crashed inside the house and Mary Margaret came out onto the porch wiping her hands on her apron. Her white hair with its faded red streaks had sort of sprung out of the small knotted bun at the back of her neck. She squinted at Julie and Father through her little round metal eyeglasses. "Not one child got off that school bus today. Not one." Mary Margaret pulled bobby pins from her hair and opened them with her teeth, patted her hair down and jabbed the pins back in, catching some of the loose ends. "'And where is Julie Kathleen?' I said to Svend. 'Where is that child?'" Mary Margaret took a breath. "Run now and get the soap and towel for your father."

Julie and her father looked at each other and rolled

their eyes.

"And you can thank the Lord for telling me to peel extra potatoes. Julie Kathleen, after you wash, you can set the table. The yellow dishes. And don't break anything, child." Mary Margaret hurried back into the house to tend to the supper.

Julie's father washed his hands and face with the hose at the back of the house. When he came into the kitchen, he was shiny and clean. His hair was wet and looked like he'd slicked it back with his hands. He winked at Julie.

Mary Margaret was fussing over the wood stove, poking at the vegetables in the pots.

"When you're finished the table, Julie Kathleen, sit yourself down. Supper will be ready in a few minutes, the Good Lord providing. Svend ... Svend! Come to the table. Duncan MacFarlane has come with Julie Kathleen to share our Lord's Blessing." "Yes, I heard." Mary Margaret's husband shuffled into the kitchen from the darkness of the living room. He always wore his floppy slippers in the house. His eyes twinkled and he picked tobacco off his lips. He was the only person that Julie knew who smoked cigarettes. He rolled his own and they were very ugly and smelly. He sat down at the table. "I saw that your crew didn't put in a full day today, Duncan. Machinery break down?"

As the men talked planting, Julie looked around the small kitchen. She counted seven pictures of Jesus hanging here and there. And many, many pictures of angels cut from magazines and old calendars. A Saint's Day calendar showing the month of May was tacked beside the fridge. Because the kitchen was so small, Svend's chair was right in front of the fridge door. When Mary Margaret needed to get something out of it, Svend had to get up and move himself out of the way.

Julie leaned down and looked under the table. She wondered if Victor was ever allowed to lie under there. The kitchen floor was pale worn linoleum and very clean. She could see Father's grey work socks and Svend's slippers. From this angle she could also see where the legs of the chairs had pressed small circle-shapes into the floor. The little dents were a rusty yellow colour. Her father gave her a nudge with his elbow and whispered, "Head's up, kiddo. Here comes the grub."

Mary Margaret put food on each person's plate over at the stove. Julie liked it better the way her mom did it, with all the bowls of food right on the table. Then you could take what you wanted. Tonight Julie poked at a yellowy clump on her plate. She leaned her face down and smelt it. Mashed turnips. Julie tapped her pointer finger against the back of Father's hand and pointed the same finger at the pile of turnips and shook her head a tiny bit. Father knew what to do. The next time Mary Margaret got up from the table—which she did a lot—Julie slid her plate over next to Father's, and he quickly scooped the unwanted food onto his plate. It didn't matter if Svend saw.

After supper Julie went out to open and swing the gate closed for her father. He had to get back home and finish fixing the tractor. She sat on the step for a few minutes. She could see where knobby green shoots had poked up out of the ground in the patch of dirt that Mary Margaret called the asparagus garden. Julie thought that was a pretty fancy name for an ordinary patch of dirt.

Victor McClusky McGlory lay at the side of the house watching her. He wasn't a bad dog but he seemed kind of sneaky, always slipping around the corner of a building or appearing when you didn't know he was around. Julie wondered if Victor didn't trust her because he wasn't used to children.

"Julie Kathleen, the Lord gave us arms and legs to make us useful. I've stacked the dishes, you come in now and finish the washing up. Children were not put on this earth to be idle."

Mary Margaret wasn't used to children either.

Chapter 10
PUFFED WHEAT CEREAL

As soon as Julie's eyes popped open in the morning, she knew she wasn't in her own room. This upstairs bedroom at Mary Margaret's was dark and so-o-o-o quiet. Julie couldn't tell if it was the right time to get up for school or not. A lonely kind of sadness tucked itself into the bed beside her. She thought about her mother and father, both away from her and away from each other.

Julie lay smack dab in the exact centre of the high, narrow bed, not even moving. She pulled the fluffy white quilt right up to her chin. "Irish feathers," Mary Margaret had told her, "like the kings of Ireland used in the old days." The room was still dark and quiet. She felt just like a queen ... or a princess ...

The small window at the end of the room lightened slowly. Julie squinted her eyes, surveying the edges of the bedroom. The dark wood ceiling sloped down from its high centre ... down ...down, then the ceiling turned into a wall, only about as tall as she was. Across from the bed along this very short wall was a small door.

Julie wondered about this door in the wall of Mary Margaret's upstairs bedroom. Even Julie would have to crouch to go through it. She would like to know what was in there. . . in the cubbyhole behind the door. There was a golden bolt, with a slider part on it, just like the one on the chicken house door at her farm. She said the word, "cubbyhole," a couple of times. A cubbyhole would be a great place to hide important things.

"Yooooo—hooooo!" Mary Margaret's high-pitched voice wound its way in zig-zigs up the staircase and into the bedroom.

Julie remembered just in time that the bed was really high off the floor, at least twice as high as her own bed at home. The first morning she stayed here, when she got out of bed, she fell right down in a heap on the braided rug on the floor. She didn't like getting out of this bed one bit. You had to turn yourself around and reach one cold bare leg way down and find the wooden stool with your toes.

Mary Margaret had given Julie a big flowered bowl and told her to put it under the bed, "… to use at night." Julie thought she knew what the bowl was for but she had NO plans to use it.

The cold floor made her gasp. A shiver tickled down her back. She put on her clothes from yesterday as fast as she could. Mary Margaret never seemed to come upstairs so Julie didn't see any reason at all to make the bed. She ran down the stairs singing, "Lazy Julie, did you get up, did you get up, did you get up?"

Mary Margaret was cooking porridge. The first morning Julie was here, she'd asked if maybe there was some Puffed Wheat Cereal. But no, Mary Margaret had said that Svend depended on her to make a good, big pot of porridge every morning. "The Blessed Lord saw fit to make the poor unfortunate creature as skinny as a fence post. Porridge sticks to his ribs and gives him substance. The Devil's breath will get no chance to twirl our Svend off his feet and blow him across the valley ... Not if he's had his bowl of porridge."

Julie just had to shake her head. She really wondered if Svend—who was very skinny when she thought about it—had ever even tried Puffed Wheat Cereal.

After breakfast, Julie went outside with her jacket on and her lunch kit swinging. Victor McClusky McGlory got up from where he was curled beside the front steps. He stretched his legs and yawned. His face was turned away from Julie as she chatted to him, "Such a handsome dog, Victor. Your black is so black and your white is so white." She knew that dogs needed a lot of compliments if they were ever going to be friendly to you. When he finished all his stretching business, Julie was pretty sure that she saw his tail wag just a titch. When she headed down the path, Victor followed her, staying back a ways ... like maybe he was going that way anyway.

Before she went through the swinging gate, she stopped and looked back at Mary Margaret's log house, remembering the cubbyhole upstairs. Victor stopped too and sat, tucking his tail around his feet. Julie frowned and saw the way the shake roof sloped way down to the edges of the house. She put her hands on her hips. The small bedroom upstairs was right in the middle of the house and its window was exactly under the peak of the roof. There must be room for a pretty big cubbyhole along the sides of the bedroom, behind those short walls.

Julie heard the sound of the school bus from away down the valley, as it changed gears so it could slow down and stop to pick up the Thompson kids. She was next. She shouted, "Goodbye, Victor. See ya' later." She had to run all the way to the road. And she did. She wanted to be there waiting at the bus stop by the mailbox when Mr. Smokey Woodburn came driving along in the big yellow bus. Maybe then he wouldn't be so darn grumpy this afternoon when she made him stop the bus and let her off at her father's place.

Chapter 11
THE SNAPSHOT

After school, Julie left the classroom and went straight outside. Some of her classmates asked her to play marbles with them but she didn't want to. Marbles seemed like a pretty silly game to be playing when her mother was a hundred miles away and she didn't know when she would see her again.

Julie stood out by the road where the school bus would stop. She folded her arms and leaned against the fence. Every day the bus driver Mr. Smokey Woodburn parked the bus for a few minutes and went into the school to chat with Miss Hendricks. Today Julie was going to ask him if she could get on the bus right away and wait there instead of in the line-up with the rest of the kids.

When the yellow school bus screeched to a halt and the door swung open the first thing that Julie saw were Mr. Smokey Woodburn's long legs. He got off the bus like he knew she would be there waiting for him.

"Julie," he said, sounding pleased for no reason at all. "Julie. I've got something for you." He scrounged his big hand around in the chest pocket of his striped grey overalls. He brought out a rather tattered piece of paper. "I had this snapshot at my place. Thought you should have it."

Julie took the paper from him and turned it over. There smiling up at her was her beautiful mother. Behind Mother, in the picture, was the school bus. And beside Mother, Mr. Smokey Woodburn himself, looking just like he always looked, same overalls. Smiling too.

Julie had seen pictures of her mother before. Up on the mantle above the fireplace at home there were framed pictures of her parent's wedding day. But they were breakable and Julie wasn't allowed to touch them.

"Someone took that snapshot when your mother first came to teach at this school, Julie. Must have been old Mr. Bell, the Superintendent. He brought a camera up when he came to inspect the school. She looks pretty young, eh?" He shuffled from one foot to the other like he was shy or something. "All those years ago. Thought you'd like it."

"Well, I do," said Julie. Her mind was racing a mile a minute. She couldn't take her eyes off the picture. And she didn't know whether she should thank him politely or hug him or cry. When she finally looked up, she saw that he was already pushing open the door to the school.

*   *   *

Today when Julie got the school bus to stop at her own farm, she realized that she should have gone straight to Mary Margaret's for once. The planting crew and the tractors were at the far end of the half planted potato field. That's where Father and Dogeez would be. She looked the other way, towards Mary Margaret's log house under the trees in the distance. "Half a mile as the crow flies," Father had told her.

Mary Margaret will want to see this snapshot of Mother, Julie thought. She got an extra good grip on the handle of her blue lunch kit, flapped her arms, and headed off across the fields. Her feet churned beneath her. Birds startled out of the grass as she raced past as fast as the wind. She skinnied under one, then another barbed wire fence. When she got to her feet and looked to see if she was still headed in the right direction, she heard barking and saw a dark streak that must be Victor coming her way from Mary Margaret's house.

As she crawled under the last fence and stood up with her feet on Mary Margaret's land, Victor was loping her way with his ears flat back against his skull. He circled her a couple times while Julie caught her breath. It seemed to Julie like he was deciding something. "C'mon, you silly mutt, let's run." Victor took off ahead of her barking.

"Mary Margaret! Look what I have! Mr. Smokey Woodburn gave it to me!" Julie was out of breath from running. She was pretty sure running was much harder than flying.

Mary Margaret was on her hands and knees in the asparagus garden, pushing dirt piles around the small shoots. As she slowly stood up, she groaned and wiped her forehead. "Oh, it's you, Julie Kathleen. I thought Victor McClusky McGlory had run off to chase coyotes away from my chicken house. Gracious Good Lord, child, you're all aflutter. Who gave you what?"

Julie and Mary Margaret sat on the steps and examined the snapshot. Mary Margaret wiped the dirt off her hands on her plaid jacket. They leaned their heads together and talked about how young Mother looked in the picture. Victor paced back and forth past the steps. Then he sat right in front of them with his head cocked to one side.

Mary Margaret gasped and pressed her hand to the top of her head. "Mary Mother of God and my own dear dead Mother have put an idea in here." She peered over the top edge of her glasses at the snapshot and measured with her thumb and forefinger. "Half an inch. Exactly." She clapped her hands together. "My County Cork trunk!" She got to her feet and went into the house.

"Come, Victor," Julie said to the dog. "See the picture?" He sprang up onto the steps and stood behind where she was sitting. "It's my mother. I don't know if you remember her. I'm sure you would like her if you knew her."

"Come along, child," Mary Margaret called. "We've work to do. Put that picture of your mother on the kitchen table."

As Julie got up, she gave Victor the quickest little pat on the head. "I have to go in now."

Mary Margaret was in her pantry banging around. She called out to Julie, "You know that size, half an inch. Look around at the angels in the kitchen. Is there one that size?"

Julie circled the room, peering carefully at the calendar pictures. For the first time ever, she really looked at them. Big fat angels draped in sheets, angels on hilltops with lambs, angels' faces peeking out of sunny clouds.

Mary Margaret came out of the pantry carrying an oil lamp. She struck a match on the stove top and lit the lamp, adjusting the wick to the right height. "Never mind the angel now, Julie. You can pick one later." Julie still didn't have any idea what was happening.

She followed Mary Margaret up the stairs and into her

own bedroom with the high white bed. Julie tried to stand between Mary Margaret and the unmade bed, just in case Mary Margaret noticed how messy it looked, but she didn't seem to pay any attention at all.

Mary Margaret said, "Can you hold this lamp steady, child?" Julie took the lamp and held it by its creaky metal handle. She could feel the warmth of the flickering flames and see the oil sloshing a little through the glass.

Mary Margaret bent over and rattled the lock on the cubbyhole door. "This is the one place I don't mind the spiders taking over." She slid the lock open. "We shan't disturb their peace." She opened the door to the cubbyhole. "Mind your step. Mind the lamp. In we go!" And with that Mary Margaret made the sign of the cross in front of her, ducked down and disappeared into the cubbyhole.

Chapter 12
THE CUBBYHOLE

Julie was left standing alone in the empty bedroom. Mary Margaret's voice sounded faint, "Bring the lamp, Julie Kathleen. It's as dark as night in here."

Julie walked slowly up to the little door. She kept her eyes as wide open as she could get them. Cool, dusty air came through the open cubbyhole door and almost made her sneeze. She held the lamp carefully in front of her and, crouching, followed its light in through the open door.

Inside the cramped cubbyhole, spider webs swayed like old grey lace. "Over here. Over here, child." Mary Margaret's voice came from the blackness beyond the lamp's yellow light. "Bring the light, hold it up high. Hang the handle over this nail. There."

Julie looked all around the cubbyhole. There were more and more spider webs every way she turned. They slid past her face and caught in her hair. Julie gave a little shriek. Spider webs gave her the heebie-jeebies.

Mary Margaret crouched over a big black box on the floor. "Help me, child. This old trunk hasn't been opened for years." Julie knelt down beside Mary Margaret and helped push the heavy lid up. With hinges squealing, the lid fell backwards and banged to a stop with a puff of dust.

The pale yellow light of the oil lamp lit the insides of the trunk. Mary Margaret was rummaging in the trunk. "Come, little spider," she coaxed. "You are no more allowed in my County Cork trunk than you are in the downstairs sitting room. You ought to know better." She held her palm up and blew gently at the spider. He wafted off into the darkness.

Julie peeked carefully inside the trunk. She could see bits of lace and cloth poking out of paper wrappings. Some books. Cards and papers tied up with strings. Mary Margaret passed her a small white box tied with white satiny ribbon. "Hold this, child. There's something else in here I'd like to find." Julie held the box out and turned it over a few times, checking for spiders. "Ah. Yes. Here it is." Mary Margaret pulled a large book from the bottom of the trunk. She smoothed tissue paper packages and mumbled words that Julie couldn't make out. Then Mary Margaret shut the lid of the trunk and crossed herself again. She held her hand against her heart. "My own sweet departed mother, God rest her soul, is in the smell of that old trunk. Lavender. It's been thirty years since she helped me pack when I left County Cork. Thirty years and now I'm older than she was when I left her behind."

Tears came to Julie's eyes. She had never even thought about Mary Margaret having a mother. She clutched the little box and the big book against her chest and when she brought her hands up to rub the tears away, she pushed spider webs all over her face and it didn't even bother her very much.

Chapter 13
THE LOCKET

Mary Margaret put the kettle on when they got back down to the kitchen. Then they both went outside and brushed the spider webs and a few spiders off their clothes. Afterwards they sat at the kitchen table waiting for the kettle to boil. "This," Mary Margaret said, patting the dusty album, "is my Irish childhood." When she opened it Julie could see pale colours and smell the teeniest whiff of perfume. "I picked these flowers from my mother's kitchen garden and from the rose garden and from the fields. On my way home from school, after church. My mother showed me how to prepare the flowers for preserving, how to press them, and how to mount them in the album."

Page after page of delicate dried flowers crinkled at Julie from behind see-through paper. Julie tried to think of how old the flowers must be and how long ago they were picked.

"Look." Mary Margaret showed Julie the few blank pages at the back of the album, "I meant to pick Canadian flowers and put them here but I never got around to it."

Mary Margaret took the dingy white box and untied the ribbon. She pulled a fine black chain up into the air and it in turn pulled up a solid black heart shape from within the box.

Mary Margaret got up quickly and brought a small blue metal container from under the sink and a raggy tea-towel back to the table. Julie knew it was the same stuff called

Silvo that they used to clean the forks and knives at her house at Christmas time. Mary Margaret opened the screw-top of the container and poured a slosh of grey liquid onto a pinched corner of the tea-towel. She rubbed at the black heart. She worked silently, rubbing and dabbing. A hard smell drifted past Julie's nose. As the rag and Mary Margaret's fingers turned black, the heart turned a bright silver colour.

At last Mary Margaret spoke. "This locket was my mother's, and she gave it to me when I left Ireland. I am now giving it to you, Julie Kathleen, because you need a proper place to keep that picture of your own dear mother." With a quick twist of her thumb nail, Mary Margaret

snapped open the locket. "Oh, Mother!" she said. "I haven't seen you for so many years. I'm much older now but you're the same." Using a finger nail, she pried the little photograph out of the locket and it fell to the table. Some dried bits of a grey-mauve flower fell out of the other side of the locket

"Now, child," said Mary Margaret turning the photograph right side up on the kitchen table. "Now we need that angel."

Julie pulled the thumb tack out of one of the calendar pictures on the wall and brought it back to the table while Mary Margaret got a pair of scissors and some paste out of a drawer. Then they set to work and managed to snip and trim both a picture of an angel and the picture of Julie's mother to a perfect size. They popped the pictures side-by-side into the silver locket.

While Julie worked on cleaning the black chain, Mary Margaret gently pasted the picture of her own mother onto the empty spot on the calendar where they had cut out the face of the angel. "I have a feeling that dear Mother will prefer being in the kitchen with me. She's been in that blessed trunk with the spiders for so many years." A smile broke out on Mary Margaret's face. "I don't suppose Mr. Smokey Woodburn would mind getting stuck with the angels either." Mary Margaret took the scissors and snipped him out of the snapshot and pasted his face smack dab in the middle of a golden cloud, surrounded by a number of angels and Mary Margaret's own mother.

Chapter 14
SUMMERTIME

It was early July and the evening was hot and muggy. Julie's father had said he could smell a thunder and lightning storm in the air. Because the school year was over, Julie was back at home with her father instead of at Mary Margaret's. Mother had been in Vancouver since the end of May, waiting to be called in for surgery. Her letters were short and always had Xs and Os for kisses and hugs in a row along the bottom of the paper. Julie read the latest letter every night before she went to bed.

Julie and her father were looking through the cupboards in the kitchen to see what they might make for supper.

"Here's a can of pork and beans. How about pork and bean sandwiches?" Julie hoped her father was kidding.

"Get out of my way, dog," Auntie Francine's voice came to them from the yard outside. "Screens keep flies out," Auntie Francine said as she let the screen door slam shut behind her and she came into the farmhouse kitchen. In her arms she carried a bag of sliced ham and buns and a big glass dish of potato salad. "I hope you didn't have anything special planned for dinner, Duncan?" She set the armful of food on the table. "Julie, be a dear and bring the ice cream from the car."

"Gee, Francine," Julie's father said, "we were just going to have ... ah ... scrambled eggs tonight."

"No more breakfasts for dinner, Duncan, dear brother.

You two need some real food." She took the ice cream from Julie and tucked it into the ice-box. "Are there any clean dishes in this house or are they all piled here in the sink?"

Julie ran outside and down the front steps. The wet coldness of the box of ice cream that she found wrapped in newspaper on the back seat of Auntie Francine's car cooled her bare arms.

After dinner, Auntie Francine pulled a *McCall's* magazine out of her big handbag. She flipped through until she came to the paper doll at the back. Then she handed the magazine to Julie. "Find some scissors, Punkin-head. Your father and I need to talk." As the adults moved into the living room with their cups of tea, Auntie Francine told Julie's father, "My boss has given me a few days off work. He's going on holidays with his family and I guess he thinks I won't have anything to do without him there directing me." She sounded cross and huffy. Julie didn't pay any more attention to them.

Julie found her old dull scissors in a box of jumbled pencils and crayons left over from school. She chewed on her lips as she concentrated on cutting out the fancy little paper doll. She wished she was allowed to use the big, sharp scissors from the sewing basket, but her mother—if she'd been here—would never in a thousand years allow Julie to use them to cut paper like this.

When she had finished cutting out the doll and all its pretty clothes, Julie flipped through the magazine until she found a bright red picture. On it she drew the shape of a small heart. As she cut out the heart she remembered to add the little flaps that are needed to hang things from doll's shoulders. She put the new heart on the doll and folded back the flaps. Then she dressed the doll in a party dress and a flowery hat. No one could even tell from just looking that the doll had a new red heart on under her clothes. Julie put the doll in her old lunch kit where she kept her mother's letters.

*   *   *

"Julie," her father said the next morning. "Francine's got it in her mind to take you on a little trip to Vancouver … to see your mother." Julie's fork dropped out of her hand and clanged onto the table. Her mouth hung open. "The train leaves at 5:30 tonight. Think we can get you ready in time?"

Julie's father went out with his tractor and mower and cut hay all morning. When he came back in for lunch, Julie was sitting on her suitcase on the porch with Dogeez keeping her company. She was already dressed in her very best clothes and wearing Mary Margaret's silver locket around her neck.

For lunch they ate lots of toast and jam and had canned peaches for dessert. "Okay, Jewels," father said after lunch, "let's take a drive over and tell Mary Margaret what's happening."

Julie sat carefully in the front of her father's truck, trying not to get her clean clothes too dusty. Mary Margaret was just washing up the lunch dishes. Svend and the haying crew were out in the field with the tractor and wagon.

"Francine and I thought Julie should go now and see her mother. I'll go later when she has the surgery."

Mary Margaret scooped leftovers into a chipped bowl. "Julie Kathleen, take the blessed scraps out to Victor McClusky McGlory, if you will, child." Julie started towards the front door, looking back at the two adults in the kitchen.

Then Mary Margaret made the sign of the cross in the air in front of her and pressed her soapy hands together, mumbling soft words and looking towards the kitchen ceiling. "Duncan MacFarlane, St. Christopher will keep her safe on this journey to see her mother."

"It's no more than four hours on the train ..."

"Yes, but you and I and the Good Lord know full well that Sophie is nearing the arms of Jesus. This will be a difficult journey for Julie Kathleen."

"Sophie will hold out, Mary Margaret. I know she will."

A scary tightness clutched at Julie's throat. She stood on the porch holding the bowl in her hand. "Victor. Victor," she called in a small voice. Victor came around the side of the woodshed and right up to Julie. He nudged her leg with his cold nose. "Victor, if they don't hurry up and do that... darn op...operation..."

Julie plunked herself down on the porch steps, forgetting about not getting dusty and forgetting that she was still holding the bowl. Through the tears that had begun to gather at corners of her eyes, she could see that Mary Margaret's asparagus garden had gone to seed. The stalks swayed in the heat like a forest of tall green feathers. Victor waited patiently, keeping his eyes on the food. Julie put the bowl down on the step beside her and threw her arms around the dog. Victor stood absolutely still. The tears trickled down Julie's cheeks, and she pushed her face against his warm neck. When she finally finished crying and let go of him, they were nose to nose. Victor didn't really have a choice. He licked her face. A couple of times. Then he leaned down and gulped the leftovers in the bowl.

When Julie's father and Mary Margaret came out of the house, Victor had already gone back behind the woodshed to lie in the shade. Julie was sitting all alone staring at the asparagus patch with the empty chipped bowl beside her.

Chapter 15
THE TRAIN TRIP

Julie leaned her back against the cool of the train seat. The train rocked her gently from side to side. It made her think of babies being rocked by their mothers. The seats were covered in a smooth, dark blue material.

"Vinyl," Auntie Francine said, touching it with her hand, "Like leather but in nicer colours. Wouldn't a vinyl sofa be splendid?" She reached for her handbag, "Here comes the conductor. Where did I put those tickets?"

Julie sat beside the window and Auntie Francine talked to a big man in a dark uniform and cap who was standing between the rows of seats. He checked over the train tickets that Auntie Francine handed him.

"Off to the big city, are we?" He winked at Julie. "Going to see the monkeys in Stanley Park?" Julie looked away from him and didn't say a word. "We'll be serving refreshments a little later," he said as he punched the tickets and handed them back to Auntie Francine. He tipped his cap to her.

Julie leaned over towards her aunt. "What's refreshments?" she whispered.

"Food." said Auntie Francine. "Sandwiches. We'll buy a snack when they bring the cart around."

There didn't seem to be anything on a train for a child to do. Julie wished that they were already in Vancouver and she could see her mother. She turned her head towards the glass of the train window. There were mostly trees and now and then some rocks in behind them. She wondered how long it was going to take to get there, but Julie's father had told her not to pester her aunt too much about how long the trip would take.

Auntie Francine stood up and took off her summer coat. As she sat back down, Julie had to ask, "When are we going to get there?"

"My word, child! We've hardly left the station."

Julie looked around the shiny train car. Even the curved ceiling was a silvery colour. The passengers had stacked their luggage on the metal rail shelves at the front of the train car. She could just see an edge of her old brown suitcase sticking out from under a stack of newer-looking ones.

"Auntie Francine?" Julie fidgeted in her seat. "Are there bathrooms on trains?"

"It's down at the back. Don't take too long, dear."

She made her way unsteadily down the aisle between the two rows of seats. She watched her feet and tried to make them walk in a straight line.

At the back of the train, Julie found a silver door that said RESTROOM in bumped-up letters across the top. The heavy door needed a big push to swing it open. When she stepped inside and let go of the door, it clanged shut and made her ears pop.

Inside the restroom, it was very cramped and smelly and the only light came from a dim bulb above the tiny sink. Her elbows bumped against the cold metal walls when she turned around. A small sign behind the low toilet said, DO

NOT FLUSH WHEN TRAIN STANDING IN STATION.

Later, after Julie found the button and flushed the toilet she could see straight down the hole to the train tracks below. A scary whooshy sound filled the room. She turned to the sink and pushed at a small pump handle. She rubbed her hands in the squirt of blue water that came out. The only thing she could find to dry her hands was a piece of rough paper in a metal holder.

Then she tried to open the door.

With her heart beating too quickly, Julie pushed and pulled at the handle, turning it every-which-way. She felt hot and needed fresh air. The door would not open.

She pounded her fists on the inside of the door and

yelled, "Help. I can't get out! Help me!"

The conductor unlocked the door from the outside with his set of keys and set Julie free. Chuckling and shaking his head, he told Auntie Francine she'd better go in with Julie next time. Her aunt gave him a very small smile and hugged Julie. Then Auntie Francine went back up the aisle to their seats, but Julie plunked herself down on an empty seat at the back of the train. She folded her arms across her chest and slumped down, scowling.

*   *   *

A sweet voice from across the aisle said, "I've probably been in that restroom a hundred times and I've never locked myself in. Haven't you ever travelled by train before?"

The girl sat alone, wearing a white lacy dress and white shoes with straps. Julie stared at her. Perfect blonde ringlets hung down either side of her thin sad face. "My name is Esme Ostoforoff. My mother and I go on this train all the time. We live in Lillooet and I take piano lessons from my maestro in Vancouver."

"You must be rich," Julie said, thinking how much train tickets cost.

"My mother says we are comfortably well-off."

Julie thought Esme sounded just like a grown-up.

"You got on the train at Pemberton," said Esme, twirling a ringlet. "I saw you. Is that your mother up there?" She pointed forward to where Auntie Francine sat.

Julie found her tongue again. "No, she's my aunt."

"We don't have any relatives. My mother and I think it

would be such a bother to have relatives." The girl fiddled with a pair of white gloves on her lap. "Come and sit with me if you wish. We are the only children on the train today, but my mother said I didn't have to talk to you if I didn't want to."

Julie moved to sit across from Esme. She smoothed down her own dress and placed her knees and feet together neatly. She touched her fingers to her silver locket.

"Who's in there?" asked Esme. "Whose picture is in your locket?"

"My mother. And an angel," said Julie and she flipped it open and leaned over so Esme could see.

"Is your mother dead?"

"No. But she's going to have an operation on her heart."

"So. She might die."

Julie looked straight at Esme and said firmly, "My father says she'll hold out."

"Well …" said Esme. Then she hummed and pretended to play the keys of a piano in the air between them. "That was Bach. The conductor's right, you know, there are monkeys in Stanley Park. My mother prefers the Rose Garden, but I like the monkeys. We always go on Sunday. Perhaps we'll see you there."

"I've never seen a monkey," Julie said.

"What's your name?"

"Julie."

"I'll call you Juliette. First, I will show you how to get that pesky restroom door to open and then I'll teach you my favorite card game." Esme pulled out a brand new deck of cards. "Well, of course," she said, "Solitaire is my favorite game ... but I do know how to play Fish."

*   *   *

After a long time playing cards, Julie went back to sit with Auntie Francine. She heard a clankety-clank coming up the aisle behind them. She turned around and knelt on her seat so she could see over people's heads. "The refreshments are coming!"

The cart was loaded down with all kinds of sandwiches, doughnuts and cookies, all wrapped up in waxy paper.

Before she'd finished her cheese sandwich, the conductor walked through the train car yelling, "Stawamus. Stawamus. Next stop."

Julie watched passengers moving about on the wooden platform. She thought of her father, waving goodbye to them from the Pemberton train station.

After Stawamus, the train wound slowly around the side of steep mountains and in and out of tunnels. Sometimes on a straight stretch, Julie could see the engine in front pulling the rest of the cars behind it, like a toy train set.

Julie's eyes followed the steep slope of the mountains all the way down to where they sank into the dark blue shimmer of water. Auntie Francine said the water was an inland arm of the the Pacific Ocean. Julie remembered about the Pacific Ocean from the big map at school that pulled down and had pictures of chocolate bars around its edges.

The sky was darkening and there was a pinkish glow in the west.

"Love these ocean sunsets," said Auntie Francine

Julie stared at the glow in the sky until all the colours faded away. Darkness fell and now she could see right into the bright living rooms of houses along the train tracks. There were tall lit-up buildings and dark paved streets on either side of the train.

"North Vancouver. North Vancouver. Last stop." The conductor walked through Julie's train car shouting. "Mind your step, ladies." He propped open the door at the front of the train car. "North Vancouver."

Passengers got up out of their seats, stretched and yawned and found their suitcases. With shudders and squeaks, the train slowed down. It crept up to the bright station and lurched to a screechy halt. People in the aisles grabbed at the back of the train seats to keep their balance.

Out on the platform, a man picked up Auntie Francine's and Julie's suitcases, one in each hand, and carried them off into the night. Auntie Francine followed the man and Julie felt so sleepy that she just trudged along without even asking any questions. The man put the suitcases in the trunk of a yellow and black car with the word TAXI lit up on its roof.

In the back seat, Julie leaned against Auntie Francine and tried to keep her eyes open. "Do you think Mother waited up for us?" Julie asked.

"Yes, I expect she has." Auntie Francine put her arm around Julie and planted a kiss on the top of her head.

*　*　*

Grandmother held her finger to her lips and shushed Julie and Auntie Francine as she let them in the front door. She closed the door behind them as they quietly set their suitcases down in the hall. Grandmother gave Julie a quick little hug and kissed her forehead without having to bend over. She pointed into the sitting room and whispered, "She's asleep."

Julie's mother sat, wrapped in afghans, in a big easy chair with her feet up on a cushioned footstool. She was just waking up. "Oh, Julie. Francine. You got here safely." She threw her arms open and Julie ran to her.

"Careful now, Julie dear," Grandmother said. "Your mother's on strict bed-rest."

"Seeing these two is the best medicine for me."

Julie sat on the arm of the chair and snuggled up beside her mother. She took big breath in through her nose. "You smell just exactly how I remember." She buried her face against her mother and said, "I've missed you every single day."

"Well," said Grandmother, coming back into the sitting room from the kitchen, where she'd flipped on the light. "Now we're all awake," she said, tying her apron strings behind her, "how about hot milk and cinnamon toast?"

Chapter 16
STANLEY PARK

"How come they call it Lost Lagoon if it's right here where we can see it?" Julie panted, pushing her mother's borrowed wheelchair along the rough sidewalk near the entrance to Stanley Park. Many other families with children were out and about on this fine Sunday in July.

"It's not lost to us," Mother told Julie. "It's lost to the ocean. This causeway, where the road is, blocked off the lagoon from the ocean. But, see, the birds love the lagoon. And swans nest out of harm's way on those little grassy islands."

Auntie Francine strolled along behind them in the sunshine, swinging her arms and humming a tune. Seagulls swooped and squawked above their heads as if they knew that Mother had a loaf of stale bread hidden under the blanket on her lap.

"Mother, do you think an albatross would be bigger than a seagull?" Julie stopped pushing and looked towards the boat-filled harbour. "Are those sailing ships? Would a sailor really go on a ship like that?"

"You are a girl-of-a-thousand-questions, Julie," Mother said laughing. "Which one should I answer first?"

Julie smiled and danced around to the front of the wheelchair. "It doesn't matter, Mother-duther. I'll just think up more." She rubbed her nose against her mother's.

When they finally got to the zoo, Julie pushed Mother's wheelchair straight up the hill through the crowds towards a building with a sign that said MONKEY HOUSE. A sharp barnyard smell wafted towards them as they got near the cages. Julie stopped and stared. A small orange-coloured monkey swung down from its perch and clutched at the bars right in front of her. The monkey pressed its wise-ancient face between the bars and blinked its amber eyes at her. It reached its arm out, trying to pinch her bare arm with its tiny brown fingers.

"Monkeys bite! Don't let it touch you, Juliette," a girl's voice piped up beside her.

Julie took a quick step back from the monkey cage. "Esme!" she shrieked. "Mother, it's Esme from the train."

The little orange monkey withdrew its hand and wrapped its fingers back around the bars of its cage. Darting

its eyes from one girl to the other, it nodded its head up and down. Up and down. Then it gave the girls a good scolding in a nattery voice and pulled its lips back, showing its pointy yellow teeth.

Esme moved in front of Julie's mother and offered her hand. "How do you do, Ma'am? I am Miss Esme Ostoforoff from Lillooet."

Mother shook Esme's hand. "Julie told me all about you, Esme. I'm glad to meet you," she said, "Where is your mother?"

"She can't tolerate the smell in here," Esme explained, waving a white handkerchief in front of her nose and sniffing. "She is waiting for me in the Rose Garden, in the shade." She twirled on tiptoes, her arms extending towards the cages. "Juliette, you must meet all the other monkeys. Priscilla has had the sweetest baby since I was here last. Come now."

The air was cool inside the enclosure and it took a minute for the girls' eyes to adjust to the shadowy light. They moved from one cage to the next, admiring the monkeys and trying to decide who belonged to whose family.

"Can't your mother walk?" Esme asked, glancing back at the wheelchair.

"Yes, of course she can. But she gets too tired."

Auntie Francine stood just outside the Monkey House. She frowned and looked back down the hill, shading her eyes from the bright sun. "Good gracious! I think that's your Grandma."

"You have a grandmother, too?" exclaimed Esme.

Outside in the bright sunlight they could see Grandma puffing her way towards them. Squirrels scattered in her path. "Shoo. Shoo. No time for you fellows today."

Julie ran down towards her. "Are you okay, Grandma?" Esme trailed behind.

Julie took Grandma's hand and held her arm the rest of the way up the hill. Esme kept pace on Grandma's other side.

At the entrance to the Monkey House they grouped around Mother, who sat quietly in her wheelchair.

"Sophie, St. Paul's Hospital called." Grandma stopped and caught her breath. "They want you to come straight away. They have a bed in the Cardiac Ward. The operation is all set for tomorrow at the crack of dawn … I've sent word to Duncan." Grandma pressed her hand to her chest, taking deep breaths. "The taxi is waiting for us."

Auntie Francine stood behind Mother's wheelchair and placed her hands gently against mother's shoulders.

"You have to leave me again, Mother." Julie crawled right onto her mother's lap, squashing the loaf of bread they had brought to give the seagulls later. She burst into tears. Mother pressed her face to Julie's and held her tight.

Esme knelt down and she patted Julie's back and looked at Mother closely. She said in her grown up voice, "You are so fortunate to have all these people around who care what happens to you." Then she nodded her head and announced, "I'm sure you'll hold out."

"Esme, you're a dear," said Mother, her tears all mixed up with Julie's. Mother smiled when she looked up and saw

Grandma holding her wrinkled-up nose with her fingers. "Grandma doesn't like the smell of the monkeys either. Give the wheelchair a push, Francine," Mother said. "We'd better go find that taxi."

As they left the entrance to the Monkey House, Julie wiped the tears from her eyes with both hands and sniffled. She could see that all the monkeys in their cages had stopped what they were doing and were watching her and her family with the greatest interest.

Chapter 17
THE MORNING OF THE OPERATION

The next morning, Julie woke before anyone else. She tugged at a big, blue satin dressing gown hanging behind the bedroom door and put it on over her pyjamas. Holding the the bottom of the dressing gown bunched up in her arms, she tiptoed down the hall past Grandma's bedroom. She moved quietly through the sitting room, past the big dark piano hunkered against the wall and out the front door. She sat in the wicker rocker on the verandah. With the dressing gown wrapped around her, she rocked back and forth, waiting for the daylight. The trees and houses on the street and even Grandma's flowers were shades of pale and dark gray. Like a colouring book before it's coloured, Julie thought. The cool morning air didn't have any Pemberton smells to it, no chicken coop or fresh cut hay.

Julie wondered if it was the crack-of-dawn yet. She shivered and rubbed her hands together to warm them. Neighbourhood cats called to one another with questions and answers that Julie couldn't understand. Once in a while the sound of a far-off car whooshed, but no cars came down Grandma's street.

At first Julie thought she just imagined that she could hear singing. She wondered if maybe Grandma was up now and had turned on the radio.

"O-o-o-o-h, what a be-e-ea-u-ti-ful mor-r-r-ning …"

No, the sound was coming from around the corner. I know that song, Julie thought. She hummed along. I know the words. She listened carefully.

"Oh, what a beau-ti-ful day. I've got a wonderful fe-e-e-e-ling. Everything's going my wa-a-a-y——ay. Everything's going my wa-a-a-a-a-a-y."

Father sings that song when he's working on the tractor. She rocked slower. He always stretches out the wa-a-a-ay word like that. Just like that.

Julie came straight up out of the rocking chair. She flew across the verandah, down the front steps and was halfway along the block headed for the singing before she knew what she was doing. She clutched the flapping dressing gown to her tummy as her bare feet slapped the concrete sidewalk.

When she got to the corner she could see her father coming towards her.

"Father, Father!" she screamed.

Father stopped, threw his canvas pack to the ground and opened his arms just in time to catch Julie.

"I knew it was you! Nobody sings like you!"

"So I've heard. Your mother says if I sing like that the chickens won't lay and the cows won't come home and the corn will cover its ears."

Julie kissed his whiskery cheek. "Where did you come from?" She stood on the sidewalk beside Father and straightened the dressing gown. Father tied the long sash properly. "Grandma said not to expect you for a few days. She thought it would take you a long time to get here."

"Couldn't see waiting days for the next passenger train. I jumped a freight. Mr. Clack phoned ahead and got the midnight freight to stop for me. Got to sit right up in the front car with the engineer." Father picked up his knapsack from the dewy grass. "I walked all the way from North Vancouver. Over there." Julie looked towards the North Shore mountains whose tops were touched by pale morning rays. "Right across the Lions Gate Bridge," he said.

Julie took his hand and they headed back toward Grandma's house. "Father, do you think it's the crack-of-dawn yet?"

Father stopped and surveyed the pale blue sky. "See that pink light over in the east?" He pointed. "That means the sun has already poked its head up over the horizon. It's officially morning now."

Julie frowned up at the brightening sky. "Well, that means Mother is ... Mother is ..." Tears gathered at the corners of her eyes.

Father knelt down in front of Julie and placed his hands on her shoulders. "That means your mother is having her operation now." He picked up a corner of the blue satin dressing gown and gently dabbed at her tears. "And that's why we're here."

Julie looked up and down Grandma's street at the green trees and bright flowers and the yellow and red and brown houses. "Look, Father," she said quietly, "all the colours have come back."

* * *

"Surely you have room for a few more, Duncan," Grandma said as she flipped the last of the pancakes on the griddle. "Have you tried my blueberry sauce?" Grandma turned towards the table where Julie sat with her father. "I was wondering the other day, Duncan, could a person put running water into that little house that was your Granny's?"

"Yup," Father said, with his mouth full. "A person could."

"Interesting," said Grandma "Such a lovely wee house."

Julie had eaten her own two pancakes with maple syrup. Pushing her plate away she watched her father with amazement.

"When did you eat last, Father?" she whispered to him.

"I can't remember," Father replied. His fork swirled a piece of pancake through the flood of blueberry sauce on his plate.

"Who's looking after Dogeez?" Julie asked.

"Svend said he'd come over and see to the livestock."

"Dogeez's not a lifestock. Dogeez is a dog." Julie hoped that Svend would talk to Dogeez nicely so he wouldn't worry about where they'd gone.

"Well," said Grandma, sliding the last stack of pancakes onto Father's plate, "I'll get these dishes washed up. I keep thinking and thinking about my poor Sophie in the very midst of that terrible operation." She opened a cupboard and put her hands on her hips. "I'm going to bake like the dickens today. That should keep me occupied."

"I know what we can do, Julie," Father said. "Let's tramp over to English Bay and count the freighters. And you can wiggle your toes in the sand. See how a real beach looks."

"After Francine gets up, she wants to get over to the library." Grandma nodded her head, "We'll all be as busy as bees."

Chapter 18
THE HOSPITAL

"Julie, have you seen St. Paul's Hospital yet?" Father asked as they held hands and waited to cross the street. "Did Granny take you there?" He knelt down beside her and pointed. "That's the back of it way over there. The red bricks. Can you see it between those buildings?" When he stood up he took Julie's hand again. "The freighters will wait …" Father said.

After a few minutes of steady walking, they came to Burrard Street and turning the corner, walked a couple

more steps to the front of the hospital. Its tall walls loomed above the little green courtyard entranceway. Cars on Burrard Street zipped by behind them.

They walked through the courtyard and up the concrete steps. Father pushed open one of the double doors and they walked into the hospital. They wasn't anyone else around. Julie felt an under-the-sink smell prickle her nose as Father read directions from a sign on the wall of the hallway. "This way to the O.R. That's the Operating Room. Maybe we can wait somewhere there." As they started down the hall Julie could hear the sound of heels tapping quickly behind them.

"Excuse me, sir. Excuse me." They both turned. A tall, older woman in a grey suit jacket and straight skirt was gaining on them. "THAT child is not allowed in THIS hospital. Didn't you read the sign? NO CHILDREN!"

"What if she was sick? Would you let her in then?" Father stood his ground and Julie ducked behind him.

"Heaven help us if she IS sick. Children are COVERED in germs. Please. Take her out."

***

"Lucky we got out of there in one piece, eh?" said Father. "Here. Here's a bench. Just what the sergeant major ordered." They sat in the courtyard on the wooden bench warm from the morning sun and looked up at the hospital. "Somewhere, behind one of those windows ... that's where your mother is."

"It's very fancy," Julie said in a small voice. She could

see rows and rows of windows along the red brick walls of the hospital. White curtains swayed in the breeze. Adults, some in white coats, hurried along the walkway in front of their bench and went into the hospital main doors through which Julie and her father had just been herded out.

"I suppose children are full of germs. You wouldn't want someone who just had an operation ..." Father counted off on his fingers, " ... getting measles or mumps or chicken pox." He ran out of diseases before he ran out of fingers.

"Did I have all those things?"

"Um-m-m-m ... I don't think so." Father stretched out his legs and crossed one foot over the other. He put his hands behind his head and yawned. "Let's sit a spell. I'm tuckered right out."

While Father rested his eyes, Julie kept watch over him. She remembered that he had been riding on a train all night and had walked a long way to get to Grandma's. He could use a little nap.

A taxicab pulled to a stop out on the street. A grey-haired woman with a hat just like Grandma's got out the back door of the taxi.

"Grandma! " Julie said when the woman looked up. As she came closer, Julie said, "There's flour on your face ..."

"Oh, fiddlesticks," said Grandma, brushing at her cheeks and fluffing her hair. "No matter. I see your poor father's conked right out. I don't suppose you've heard anything yet." Grandma sat down on the bench beside Julie and pulled yarn and knitting needles out of her bag. "I've left the bread to rise. I had nothing else to do."

Auntie Francine's high heels clicked on the sidewalk as she walked towards them. She was looking down, frowning at her wristwatch.

"My, my. Look who else has arrived!" said Grandma.

This time at the sound of Grandma's voice, Father opened his eyes and looked around.

Auntie Francine saw them all lined up on the bench. "Great minds think alike," she said and came to a stop. "Peas in a pod." She smiled at the three of them. "Of course, I should have known the library wouldn't be open this early. Got room for one more?"

Julie got up and squiggled into the little space on the other side of Father. Grandma slid over and then there was lots of room.

Father rubbed his eyes and ran his fingers through his already tousled hair. He took his pocket watch out and checked the time.

"We'll know soon," he said, slipping the watch back into his pants pocket. "Julie, you hold the fort here with Grandma and Francine." He got to his feet and smoothed his pants with his hands and tucked in his shirt.

As Julie sat looking up at him, she couldn't think of any words to say.

"We'll know soon," he said again as he turned and strode towards the main doors of the hospital.

Chapter 19
GETTING THE NEWS

When Father came back out of the hospital this time, his face was white and his voice shaky. He said to Julie and Grandma and Auntie Francine who had all risen to their feet, "There's a complication. That's all they'll say."

Julie threw herself at her father and they clung to each other. Auntie Francine took Grandma by the arm and sat her back down on the bench.

Father continued, "They aren't telling me what it is. I … ah … I have to stay near her." He picked Julie right up off her feet in a hug so fierce she could hardly breathe. Then he set her back down. "You folks go on home." He turned toward the hospital and stopped, "I'll telephone you. I promise. When I hear."

Auntie Francine was making the return trip by train to Pemberton the next day and she decided to continue with her plan to take out some books from the public library. Julie and Grandma walked slowly back to Grandma's house—hardly saying a word—dawdling along the way, looking into shop windows on Robson Street. They stopped for tea and crumpets at a bakery shop and took a long time to get home.

When Grandma finally turned the key in her back door and they let themselves into her kitchen, they found the bread dough that she had set to rise had puffed up tremendously and spread all out of the pan and over the counter. A big blob of it had slopped onto the floor. "Oh, gracious,"

Grandma said, collapsing into a chair. "What next?"

The black wall telephone rang shrilly. Julie jumped and looked at Grandma. Clearing her throat, Grandma rose from her chair. She smoothed her curly hair. Her eyes met Julie's as the telephone rang again.

Grandma picked it up and spoke quietly. Her eyes filled with tears as she listened, then she held the receiver for Julie, "It's for you, dear. It's your father."

Julie could feel her heart pounding against her chest. She felt cold and hot at the same time. It felt as though there was too much air in her head. She took the telephone receiver and held it against her right ear like Grandma had held it. "Hello," she said, not sure how loud she was supposed to speak.

"Hey, toots!" said Father, shouting and sounding just like Father. "Your mother's okay. She's all right. I've just seen her. I'll be sticking around here, they're going to let me sit right outside her door. Just wanted you to know that in the end she came through like a charm."

After Julie carefully hung up the black telephone, she couldn't remember if she had said goodbye to Father or said anything at all to him. Grandma had sat back down and her shoulders were shaking and tears were running down her cheeks. But it looked like she was laughing.

"Grandma?" Julie said. "Are you … are you … fine? Are you …?"

"Oh, Julie, doll," said Grandma, sobbing and laughing at the same time. "Your mother made it through that dreaded heart surgery … and I forgot about the silly bread dough, and it's all over the kitchen! It just goes to show what is really important." Grandma reached over and flapped her hand against the pale puffy dough on the counter. "Messy kitchens don't matter two-hoots!"

At bedtime Julie tossed and turned, she just couldn't get comfortable and fall asleep. It was well after dark by the time Father came back to Grandma's. He peeked into the room that Julie shared with Auntie Francine and blew a kiss. Julie could see his outline in the light from the living room behind him. He made the 'thumbs up' sign. Then Julie fell fast asleep.

Chapter 20
THE DAY AFTER THE OPERATION

In the morning, Father told Julie and Grandma that Mother was hooked up to every gadget imaginable and that one of the machines actually showed each beat of her heart on a screen that he could watch.

"Her heart's working like a charm," he said. "It's the incision that will take some time to heal, they tell me. It goes from the middle of her chest around her side and part way up her back. It must be 20 inches long." He traced an imaginary line from his front to his back. "The nurses told me that the surgeons would have had to break her ribs to get at her heart." Hearing this made Julie want to put her hands over her ears.

She stayed put at Grandma's while Father went to sit by Mother's bedside at the hospital.

"Grandma," said Julie, while she waited for breakfast to be served. "I've had my whole head full of worrying about Mother. And now it feels kind of empty. I don't know if I need to worry now. Or not." Julie wasn't sure what exactly what she was trying to tell Grandma.

"Indeed," said Grandma. "That is just how I feel." She sat down at the table with Julie even though the toast had popped and was waiting to be buttered. "I think I will worry just a little longer, until she's back on her feet." Grandma reached over and touched Julie's cheek. "Just a wee bit longer."

Grandma settled Julie on the sofa and rounded up

coloured paper and a box of crayons, scissors and glue. Julie
had seen get well cards in a stationer's shop on Robson
Street and she wanted to make enough cards for Mother so
that she would get one every day that she was in the hospital. Julie arranged all the card-making supplies on the coffee
table in front of her and set to work.

Julie had noticed that there was a small black television
set in Grandma's sitting room, draped with a white cro-
cheted doily. Grandma said that she had recently purchased
the set at the Woodwards store and had hardly turned it on.

After lunch Grandma checked the newspaper and said,
"Well, there's something on called Fun-O-Rama. Cartoons."
Grandma clicked a dial on the television, "You mustn't stare
at the screen for more than a few minutes at a time, darling,
or you'll do harm to your eyes."

Julie wasn't sure exactly what harm to your eyes meant
and she didn't ask.

The television screen had blinked on and a black and
white picture came slowly into focus. Julie immediately forgot that she was not supposed to stare. The cartoons were
mostly about animals who talked and chased each other
around and around and got in trouble. A cat and a mouse
and bird and a coyote. It was extra funny when the chaser
got in trouble and fell off a cliff or had a vase fall on his
head.

After the Fun-O-Rama show was over, Grandma came
in and said, "I heard you laughing out loud, dearie." She
went over to the television set and placed her hand on the
top of the doily. "My goodness. The set has heated right

up." Grandma clicked off the television and picked up the warm doily. "Mustn't take chances. You just never know with these new fangled contraptions." Grandma set the doily on the coffee table. "I certainly hope you haven't strained your eyes."

"They're fine, Grandma," said Julie and she waited until Grandma left the room before she rubbed her stinging eyes. She went back to making cards for Mother.

Later when Father came back to Grandma's he told Julie, "Your mother opened her eyes today ... I'm sure she did ... She saw me kissing her hand." Father grinned at Julie as she held open Grandma's front door for him. "Of course, the way Dr. Pardon makes me dress up in those green hospital robes and that mask covering my face, she'd be hard pressed to know it was me doing the kissing."

"Oh Father," said Julie, shaking her head at him. "You're the only one who'd be kissing her!" Tugging at her father's hand, she pulled him into the sitting room. "Look, I've been making cards for mother, but then I took a little break to watch Fun-O-Rama on the television and now Grandma is letting me watch the Roy Rogers Show. You should see him! He's got a horse called Trigger."

Father munched on the sandwich that Grandma brought him and paid attention while Julie sorted through the jumble of crayons and pieces of papers on the coffee table in front of them. They both looked up now and then and watched the television show. Julie showed him every single one of Mother's cards. There was one with a cat on top of a television with a doily for a hat and smoke curling out of its ears. And another with a skinny coyote spread out like a pancake at the bottom of a canyon. And a cat flying on a very small airplane with mice for passengers.

"Mother will be feeling pretty sick at first," she explained to father, "and would really like the cards with pictures of flowers and nice sayings. Then when she starts to feel better she'd need more interesting cards to look at. Look, this is Dogeez and Victor talking about how they want Mother to come home soon." Julie plucked the white doily out from under a jar of glue paste and placed it daintily on the top of the television set. "Grandma says there's no point in really cleaning up until I'm all finished." She screwed the lid onto the glue jar. "Did you notice, Father, that everyone else drives a car but Roy Rogers rides that palomino horse?"

Chapter 21
DOUBLE SURE

Three days after Mother's surgery, Father and Julie sat with Grandma at her kitchen table. Grandma had served tea in fancy china cups with matching saucers and there were tiny silver teaspoons to stir the sugar and milk into the tea. Grandma was knitting now but her needles were not clicking as fast as usual. Father had just been to a meeting at the hospital with Dr. Pardon and the heart surgeon. They had told him that although Mother was recuperating from her surgery as well as could be expected, she would need to stay in hospital for some time.

Father told Julie and Grandma, "Well, of course. They want to be double sure she's fine before they send her home. They know how far it is to Pemberton. And they know there's no doctors in our neck of the woods." Father's shoulders sagged and he leaned his elbows on the table.

Julie swallowed hard but a lump stayed in her throat. "She's been away so long already," she said quietly.

"How can we leave her, Granny?" He rubbed both of his rough hands over his face and breathed deeply. "Just doesn't seem right—going back home and leaving Sophie in that hospital."

"Duncan," said Grandma, reaching over and patting his arm. "I'll be at that hospital every day visiting with her. I'll make sure she's being taken care of properly."

"It's ... so-o-o hard to leave without her."

Julie stared across the table at Father. A big tear slid

down the side of his cheek and headed for his chin. Julie froze and stared at the tear. She couldn't move. Her heart banged in her chest. The tear slipped its way down and further down.

Julie wanted to grab one of the teaspoons and leap up from her chair and dash around the table to Father's side. She couldn't move. She kept her eyes on the tear on Father's face. Then there was another one. She wanted to scoop up his tears with the teaspoon like he did for her when she cried. But she still couldn't move. She stayed stuck in her chair staring at Father. Tears gathered at the corners of her own eyes.

Grandma had risen from her chair and turned away dabbing at her face with a corner of her apron. "I'll write to you every week," she said. "Sophie can send notes along when she's able. And of course there's Julie's get well cards to take to her."

The lump was still stuck in Julie's throat. She made herself walk to the living room and gather up the cards from the coffee table. Back at the kitchen she started to count them into piles of ten. Before she opened her mouth she wondered if she would be able to talk. "How many, Father?" Her voice did work after all. "How many does Mother need for one-a-day?"

Father smiled at her and wiped his hands across his cheeks. He cleared his throat. "Until the doctors are double sure? My guess is that's a month or so. Maybe two." His finger traced the lacy cut-out heart that Julie had pasted to the front of one of the cards. "This is ... let's see ... the middle of July. If you had 60 cards that would get us to potato digging time, somewhere around mid-September."

"Sixty cards!" Julie gasped. "I'll be in Grade Six by September! I'll be nearly grown-up!"

"It's a perfect time for your mother to come home." Father smiled at Julie. "She loves that time of year on the farm." He turned to Grandma. "It's so beautiful in the fall. In the morning the mist comes right down and hunkers along the tops of the fence posts. Then the sun burns it away and you can see that all the trees on the mountains have turned colour. You'll come, Granny, won't you? I mean, you'll come home with Sophie when she gets out of hospital?"

"Of course, I'll come, Duncan. Sophie will need my help."

"No, I mean ... will you come and live with us?" Father's eyes sparkled and the corners of his mouth pulled into a smile. He crooked his finger at Julie. This time her legs did what she wanted them to do. She moved around to his side. They stood and faced Grandma across the table. "Go ahead, Julie," he whispered.

"On behalf of the MacFarlane family, I cordi ... cordi ..."

"Cordially," said Father quietly.

"I cordially invite you to come and live in Pemberton. With us." Julie let out a big breath of air.

Grandma set down her knitting and folded her hands on her quilted placemat. She looked around her kichen, then at Julie and Father. She was silent a moment, then said, "I'll consider your offer." She pursed her lips. "It's a big decision to make. I'd have to have my own house, you know. I've been independent for too many years now."

"Well," said Father, "I'm sure we can work something out." He winked at Julie. "That old house on our property is soundly built. It just needs running water. And electricity. And a good cleaning out. New coat of paint. Windows replaced. Walls moved around." He winked again. "No problem at all."

Julie remembered how her Grandmother had looked twirling around in the dusty kitchen of the empty old house at the bottom of their garden. She nodded to him knowingly and went back to counting Mother's get well cards.

Chapter 22
THE RENOVATION

Every single week for the rest of the summer, a letter came by mail from Grandma all the way from Vancouver to Pemberton. Julie got to know the clunky sound of the mail truck coming up the road. And she almost got used to the loud screeching sound the lid of their old mailbox made when she peeked inside to see if there was a letter.

In one of the first letters Grandma had printed:

Your mother is fine and dandy. She is onto solids now and talking up a storm with that Mrs. Crosby with the gall stones. Duncan, please send me the room measurements of the old house. I must choose which furniture to have shipped up on the train. Although it will be difficult to transport I am bringing my old piano.

Mother's notes were tucked in with Grandma's letters:

Darlings, I am feeling so much better. I miss you both tremendously.

During the week Father was very busy with the summertime farm work. When the haying started, Father spent a few minutes every morning before he left the house cutting the loaves of bread into slices. Then it was easier for Julie to put together sandwiches for the crew's lunch. When Julie cut the bread herself, the slices ended up all crooked, like wedges, skinny on top and fat at the bottom. Julie took the sandwiches and juice out to the haying field in a metal bucket. After lunch Father drove the tractor that pulled the hay wagon, and Julie and Johnson Jackson and the rest of the crew rode on the very top of the huge pile of hay as the wagon made its slow creaky trip from the field to the barnyard. Julie lay flat on her back on the spongy, prickly hay and watched the clouds above her change their shapes in the bright blue sky. Dogeez trotted alongside. He wasn't allowed on the wagon because he wouldn't stay put like Julie.

When the hay was all in the barn, Father rogued the potato field, pulling out the plants that didn't look healthy. Julie and Dogeez walked along with him, each in their own separate row. Dogeez wasn't very good at sticking to his row. He jumped back and forth. Sometimes he took off running and went all the way to the end of the row before he turned and came back. Then his tongue hung out and he panted.

Once in a while Father would stoop and pull out a sick-looking potato plant. He would kneel then in the soft brown earth, scoop out all the tiny potatoes and put them in a sack he had slung over his shoulder.

When Mary Margaret and Svend heard that Julie's Grandma was planning to move to Pemberton in the fall, they offered to come and lend a hand with the renovations on the old house. There was a lot of work to do before the old house would be ready for Grandma to live in.

On the first Saturday that they started the work, Julie went out onto the porch when she heard the Sorenson's truck doors slam. Dogeez bounded up from his shady spot on the porch and almost knocked Julie over as he ran, barking, to check on the vistors and especially to check on Victor.

"Fiddlesticks," Julie said, trying Grandma's word as she caught her balance. She followed Dogeez.

Mary Margaret was in the back of the truck fussing around gathering up some things, a basket and a crate it looked like, and handing them to Svend. "Out of my way Mr. Victor McClusky McGlory," Mary Margaret warned the dog.

Victor jumped out. Dogeez ran straight up to him. Victor froze. The hair on the backs of their necks bristled. Dogeez circled, growling menacingly. Victor stood stock-still, holding his ground. They both showed their teeth.

Julie could hear Mary Margaret scolding the dogs, "I have never in all my born days witnessed such dreadful behaviour. Mary Mother of God, I am ashamed of the two of you. The child is at her wit's end with worry about her poor-sick-mother, and you two act like this. You foolhardy louts shan't get a scrap of my roast beef if you keep this up. Not a sacred scrap!"

The dogs both flicked their gaze up at Mary Margaret in the back of the truck.

"Come on, you guys," Julie said, moving slower as she came closer to the snarling dogs. "Don't fight. It makes me so sad." And saying that she sat down on the gravel of the driveway and burst into tears. She pushed her hands against the front of her face and sobbed.

"Now look what you've done," Mary Margaret said, still talking to the dogs as, with Svend's guidance, she hurriedly clambered down from the tail gate.

By the time Mary Margaret and Svend bustled around the side of their parked truck and got to where Julie was sitting on the ground, both of the dogs were already there, licking at Julie's face and hands and nudging her ears with their noses. The dogs bumped into each other and into Julie and nearly pushed her over. She sobbed some more and then the Sorensons could hear her giggle, then a little sob, then another giggle.

"Don't tickle my ears!" Julie pushed at the dogs' snouts. She pulled the neck of her t-shirt up over her face and rubbed away the dog slobber. Her sobs had stopped for good. Julie flopped an arm over each of the dogs and got to her feet. "I think we're okay now," she said with a hiccup. She turned and walked towards the house, sniffling. The dogs followed her, Dogeez first, then Victor close behind. Mary Margaret and Svend didn't say a word as they trailed Julie and the dogs up to the house.

Dogeez flopped out at the edge of the porch where he could keep an eye on Victor who chose a spot at the bottom of the steps. Mary Margaret walked around him but Svend stepped over him. In the kitchen they put down the wicker basket and the crate that they had brought in. Then Svend went off to find Father who was already down at the old house.

"The Lord has blessed me with a good hammer-arm," said Mary Margaret to Julie. She unpacked a loaf of brown bread and cold roast beef from the basket onto Julie's kitchen counter. "And Svend is small enough to be very useful in crawl spaces when there is plumbing to be dealt with." Mary Margaret sliced off a couple of crispy roast beef edges and set them aside for the dogs.

Julie found the latest letter from Grandma and read it out loud to Mary Margaret:

Sophie has been started on a program of physical therapy. The nurses already have her getting out of bed and walking to the washroom. They say the sooner up after heart surgery, the better. Of course, they are always there to assist. They treat her like a princess.

Mary Margaret clucked her tongue in agreement as she rummaged under the sink for cleaning supplies to add to what she already had in the small wooden crate. "She'll be back before we've had time to count our blessings," she said as she passed Julie a bottle of vinegar, clean torn rags, steel wool and a couple of Fuller Brush Man scrub brushes.

"She'll be back in September, Father says."

Mary Margaret opened the screen door and tossed the roast beef to the dogs who gobbled without chewing. Then she hauled a bucket of warm sudsy water out of the sink and tucked the broom and mop under her arm. Julie lifted up the wooden crate and balanced it like firewood in her arms. She held the screen door open with her foot until Mary Margaret got through safely. They avoided stepping on Victor at the bottom of the step and staggered down the path with their loads and into the old house.

Father and Svend were already making plans to add a lean-to, just large enough for a toilet, sink and bathtub. Father scratched his head, "Somehow or other the plumbing will need to be rigged-up through here." He pointed to the kitchen wall.

"Mary Margaret would probably be happy to tell us how to do it, Duncan," Svend said quietly.

"Our own dear departed grandmother, Duncan, would have given her right arm for indoor plumbing when she lived here," said Mary Margaret putting down the slopping bucket. "Remember bringing her snow to melt on that wood stove?"

"Did you and Father have the same grandmother, Mary Margaret?" asked Julie.

"That's how we got to be cousins." Mary Margaret had started sweeping. Dust rose. "I was sent out from Ireland to care for our ailing grandmother. Thirty years ago now. I lived here in this little house with her for five years before she passed on and Svend Sorenson came along on his noisy motorcycle."

Julie tried to sort this out in her mind. "Where was Father? Was he here too?"

Mary Margaret stopped sweeping and remembered. "Yes, indeed. Just a bit of a boy with pink cheeks and scraped-up knees. The apple of our grandmother's eye." She made the sign of the cross. "God rest her soul." She swept her broom over to where the men were standing. "If the Lord's willing, Duncan, there's no earthly reason why we can't run the water pipe through the wall right there." Mary Margaret passed her broom to Svend. "Come, I'll show you," she said to Father.

"I told you she had it all figured out," said Svend, in his gentle voice, wagging his finger at Mary Margaret as she moved into the next room. Father shrugged and followed her.

Julie had plunked the wooden crate of cleaning supplies on the floor. She put her hands on her hips and watched Svend as he leaned the broom against the wall and pulled out his pouch of tobacco and rolling papers.

"You had a noisy motorcycle?" she asked.

"Ya," said Svend and then he licked his tongue along the edge of the paper in his hands that held a long brown strip of tobacco. "That's why Mary Margaret fell for me." He stepped out the door and lit a match with his thumb nail. "Hook, line and sinker." He smiled to himself but Julie could still see him.

Chapter 23
BACK TO SCHOOL IN SEPTEMBER

Julie lined up her brand new school supplies on the kitchen counter. She tried to remember if she had everything she would need for Grade Six. A couple of scribblers, Elmer's School Glue, 3H pencils, pencil crayons, wax crayons and a Pink Pearl eraser. She changed her mind and stacked everything in a tidy pile with the little box of wax crayons on the very top.

Somehow the list that Miss Hendricks had given out in June had been lost. Father had taken Julie down to the Valley Food Mart to get her school things and they just had to guess what she might need. Mother would have known exactly what to get, Julie thought, because she used to be a teacher and all.

Auntie Francine came to cook a macaroni and cheese casserole for Julie and her father for supper that night. She unpacked groceries out of brown paper bags. She smoothed Julie's hair down with her hand, frowning a bit. "Next weekend I'll make you an appointment with my hairdresser. A little trim wouldn't hurt. Maybe some nicer ... bangs ... "

After they had finished eating and pushed their plates back, Auntie Francine passed a paper bag to Julie. "Here, Little Miss Toots, see if you like this."

Julie reached deep into the bag. "Jeepers," Julie said and pulled out a bright red lunch kit that she put on the table to admire. On the front of the metal lunch kit were coloured pictures of Roy Rogers and Trigger.

"Open it up."

Julie unlatched the lid and plucked out a piece of folded-up cloth. It had two straps and a picture of a rearing-up Trigger printed right on its front. Auntie Francine was almost as excited as Julie. "It's a book bag for school. Your Grandma told me how much you liked the Roy Rogers Show on television."

When Auntie Francine left, she ruffled Julie's hair. "I won't forget to make the hair appointment, honey. We'll get you all beautied-up for when your mother comes home. Good luck in Grade Six."

* * *

The next morning Julie waited impatiently for the school bus. Dogeez sat quietly beside her, keeping her company. Finally the bus came chugging along the road towards her, puffs of dust following along behind. "Goodbye, Dogeez. See 'ya after school," Julie called as she clambered up the bus steps, holding her new Roy Rogers lunch kit carefully in one hand and clutching the Trigger book bag full of school supplies in the other.

Mr. Smokey Woodburn smiled at her. "Good to see you, Julie. I hear your mom's doing really good."

"She sent us a letter. She's coming home in a few weeks."Julie told him.

Mr. Smokey Woodburn kept smiling. And talking. "Guess what? I hear that it's not Miss Hendricks this year. It's a Mrs. Somebody-or-Other.

Julie stopped right where she was and stared at him. "Not Miss Hendricks! What do you mean not Miss Hen-

dricks?" Julie stomped to the first empty seat and plunked herself down. "That's the worst thing I ever heard!" All the children on the bus were already a-buzz talking about this new teacher whose name they didn't even know.

When the bus stopped in front of Pemberton Meadows Elementary, Julie was the first off. She ran through the gate and up the steps two at a time and in the front door. The rest of the children were right behind her. Even the bus driver got off and followed them into the school.

There were already a few children seated at desks in the classroom, the ones that lived nearby and didn't need to take the bus. They turned, smiling secretively, and watched Julie and the other children crowd into the back of the classroom.

There seated at the teacher's desk, just like always, was Miss Hendricks. She smiled her biggest, most beautiful smile. She rose when she saw the children and picked up a piece of chalk and printed on the blackboard:

Mrs. Woodburn.

"Mr. Woodburn and I got married!" said Miss Hendricks. "I'm Mrs. Woodburn now!"

The children's mouths dropped open and they turned and stared at the bus driver standing behind them leaning in the doorway to the classroom. Mr. Smokey Woodburn shrugged his shoulders and said, "Tricked you good, didn't I?"

*   *   *

After the classroom settled down and the children were all seated in their grade groups and busy admiring their new readers, Mrs. Woodburn called Julie up to her desk.

"You've had quite a summer, Julie. What with your mother away and all. I hear she'd doing very well. And expected back soon!"

"Mother told us in a letter that she'll be home before the snow flies. I went to Vancouver, you know." Julie gave Mrs. Woodburn a big hug, "I'm so glad you're still you. And I saw monkeys in Stanley Park and got locked in the bathroom on the train. I had a lot of fun. A girl called Esme taught me how to play Fish. But it doesn't have anything at all to do with fish."

"Oh, Esme! Of course, you are the Juliette in the letter. Look what came for you." Mrs Woodburn pulled open her desk drawer and searched around.

"What?" said Julie. "What is it?"

"This letter came for you in care of the school." Mrs Woodburn handed an envelope to Julie.

Across the front of the envelope was printed:

> Miss Juliette
> c/o Pemberton Meadows Elementary School
> Pemberton
>
> British Columbia

On the back of the envelope in the same perfect printed letters it said:

> Miss Esme Ostoforoff
> General Delivery
> Lillooet
> British Columbia

Julie shrieked, "It's from Esme!"

Mrs. Woodburn showed her how to open the envelope with her pointed letter opener.

Esme wrote:

My dearest Juliette, my mother and I would like to inquire as to the health of your beautiful mother. I am also curious as to how your sweet Grandmother and your lovely Aunt are keeping. I hope your father is well also. I am sending you a page out of my Teaching Little Fingers to Play *beginner's piano* book. *The piece is from Handel and a good place to start your musical education. You will need to find a piano that you can use. Because you will need to practice.*

I eagerly await your reply to this letter.

Your pen pal,
Miss Esme Ostoforoff

Chapter 24
MOTHER COMES HOME

It was the middle of September and a cool morning mist hung over the potato field. The tops of the plants had been rototilled in preparation for harvesting. The digging crew was set to arrive after breakfast. Father told Julie that he was anxious to see how the crop came up out of the ground.

"It's a wait-and-see game every year with the potatoes." He paused. "It was sort of the same with your mother's operation, wasn't it?" Father was over at the stove cooking up a big mess of scrambled eggs and potatoes for breakfast. "And that turned out well, didn't it?" He hummed as he scraped and flipped.

Julie was dawdling. She hadn't even made a sandwich for her school lunch yet. "Can I count in days yet, Father? Or is it still weeks before Mother will be home?"

"Well," Father said, considering Julie's question, "she said she'd be here by the end of September in her last letter. That's two weeks. About fourteen days. Three hundred and some odd hours. Give or take a few." He scooped eggs and potatoes out of the frying pan and slid a plateful across the table to Julie. He passed her a fork and knife and the bottle of ketchup. "She'll be home in the blink of an eye." They both picked up their forks and stirred the food and ketchup around on their plates.

"But we're not finished with Grandma's house yet. There's all those curls of wood on the kitchen floor, and the sink and the tub need cleaning out, the windows are still dirty and the ..."

"Yes, yes," Father said, "but Granny knows it's potato digging time. And we can't stop 'til they're all piled up in the root house. We'll get the little house finished off. Not to worry, Julie-Dooley." Father glanced at the kitchen clock. The digging crew would be here soon. Julie had some time to wait before the school bus was due.

"Mary Margaret's going to bring over some baking for our coffee-break. Bless her heart," Father said fondly as he picked up their empty plates and pushed his chair back from the table. "Somehow we're managing but we'd rather your mother was home, wouldn't we?"

***

That afternoon, on the ride home on the school bus, Julie thought up a good way to tease Mr. Smokey Woodburn for the trick that he had played on her and his other little bus riders. She was almost used to calling the teacher Mrs. Woodburn but today when she skipped her way off the school bus she called out, "Good night, Mr. Smokey Hendricks!

"Good night, Julie-Scallywag-Macfarlane." The bus driver chuckled as he swung the school bus door open.

Julie saw that the mail box was turned out which meant there had been a mail delivery. Even when the mail box wasn't turned out she always checked. If there was a letter from mother, she didn't want to miss it.

Julie grabbed the letter out of the mailbox and ripped it open. Dogeez waited for her on the other side of the road. He woofed a little sound and wiggled in an excited sort of dog-way, but Julie couldn't tell why.

She read the letter from Mother as she walked towards the house:

Dear Duncan and Julie.

Great news. Dr. Pardon is sending me home much earlier than expected. There has been an outbreak of Staph Infection at the hospital. He said I would be far better off back in Pemberton. So Grandmother and I will be coming on the train as soon as possible.

Julie crunched the letter in her fist and ran as fast as she could towards the house. Where's Father, she thought. I've got to find him and tell him Mother's coming home. She stopped. He might be in the potato field. Or the root house Julie felt all dithery and couldn't make up her mind which way to run. "Dogeez, help me," she shrieked, almost in tears. Dogeez bounded on towards the house and up onto the porch. Julie followed him and threw open the front door.

Mother and Father were sitting at the kitchen table. Just like before.

Janet Miller grew up on a farm in Pemberton, B.C. She has jumped out of an airplane, worked in an oil rig camp kitchen, pulled lumber on a green chain, managed a clothing factory in Mexico with disabled adults for over twenty years. Janet likes Cuban music and peppermint tea. She lives with her husband and two children on the Sunshine Coast in B.C. She writes short fiction and stories for children, this is her first novel.

Illustrator Martin Rose is a Vancouver film-maker and illustrator. His films have included *Trawna Tuh Bevul* for the National Film Board of Canada as well numerous independent productions. Martin is currently working on the production of *Slip*, his own independent film for which he received a Canada Council Grant. Martin teaches animation at the Emily Carr Institute of Art & Design. This is his second Hodgepog book.

If you liked this book...
you might enjoy these other Hodgepog Books:
For grades 5–8

Into the Sun
By Luanne Armstrong, illustrated by Robin LeDrew
ISBN 0-9686899-9-X $8.95

Read these yourself in grades 3–5,
or read them to younger kids

Ben and the Carrot Predicament
by Mar'ce Merrell, illustrated by Barbara Hartmann
ISBN 1-895836-54-9 $4.95

Getting Rid of Mr. Ributus
by Alison Lohans, illustrated by Barbara Hartmann
ISBN 1-895836-53-0 $6.95

A Real Farm Girl
By Susan Ioannou, illustrated by James Rozak
ISBN 1-895836-52-2 $6.95

A Gift for Johnny Know-It-All
by Mary Woodbury, illustrated by Barbara Hartmann
ISBN 1-895836-27-1 $5.95

Mill Creek Kids
by Colleen Heffernan, illustrated by Sonja Zacharias
ISBN 1-895836-40-9 $5.95

Arly & Spike
by Luanne Armstrong, illustrated by Chao Yu
ISBN 1-895836-37-9 $4.95

A Friend for Mr. Granville
by Gillian Richardson, illustrated by Claudette Maclean
ISBN 1-895836-38-7 $5.95

Maggie & Shine
by Luanne Armstrong, illustrated by Dorothy Woodend
ISBN 1-895836-67-0 $6.95

Butterfly Gardens
by Judith Benson, illustrated by Lori McGregor McCrae
ISBN 1-895836-71-9 $5.95

The Duet
by Brenda Silsbe, illustrated by Galan Akin
ISBN 0-9686899-1-4 $5.95

Jeremy's Christmas Wish
by Glen Huser, illustrated by Martin Rose
ISBN 0-9686899-2-2 $5.95

Let's Wrestle
by Lyle Weis, illustrated by Will Milner and Nat Morris
ISBN 0-9686899-4-9 $5.95

A Pocketful of Rocks
by Deb Loughead, illustrated by Avril Woodend
ISBN 0-9686899-7-3 $5.95

Logan's Lake
by Margriet Ruurs, illustrated by Robin LeDrew
ISBN 1-9686899-8-1 $5.95

Papa's Surprises
by Constance Horne, illustrated by Mia Hansen
ISBN 0-9730831-1-5 $6.95

Fuzzy Wuzzy
by Norma Charles, illustrated by Galan Akin
ISBN 0-9730831-2-3 $6.95

And for readers in grade 1-2,
or to read to pre-schoolers

Sebastian's Promise
by Gwen Molnar, illustrated by Kendra McCleskey
ISBN 1-895836-65-4 $4.95

Summer With Sebastian
by Gwen Molnar, illustrated by Kendra McClesky
ISBN 1-895836-39-5 $4.95

The Noise in Grandma's Attic
by Judith Benson, illustrated by Shane Hill
ISBN 1-895836-55-7 $4.95

Pet Fair
by Deb Loughead, illustrated by Lisa Birke
ISBN 0-9686899-3-0 $5.95